Sustenance

Elizabeth Wassell

LIB
ERT
IES

This book is for
Seamus O'Connell,
chef extraordinaire,
some of whose dishes
are described in these pages

and for

Dave Caffrey
(1947–2007)
his splendid table, from Allihies to Paris

The author thanks the following for their invaluable culinary advice: Sharon Jones, Fr Ken Letts, Sibyl Montague, Birgitta Saflund, Sean Sweeney and Paolo Tullio.

Special thanks to Dick F., Linda P., and Dan B.
And to J. M., as always.

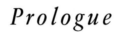

Prologue

My grandfather, who had once been a ballet dancer, lived in a jewel casket of an apartment near Carnegie Hall. He had plundered the theatres to furnish his rooms: a crimson canopy billowed above his bed; all kinds of properties, from scimitars to tasselled shawls, decorated the walls. There were pictures of Nijinsky and Tamara Karsavina and himself as a golden young man dancing for Balanchine. A burnished samovar commanded the kitchen. Whenever I visited him he served me caviar, black bread and strong tea in a glass, and, later, when I was considered old enough, chilled vodka in a tiny pewter cup.

With his stories, my grandfather spirited me to White Russia, to willowy ballerinas and temperamental choreographers, to banquets at the Russian Tea Room where ageing dancers wept on Balanchine's shoulder and young dancers were toasted with glasses of vodka, to dressing rooms full of the slightly disgusting smell of sweat mingled with face powder, to rivalries, love affairs, hours of practice, to bruised limbs and deformed feet concealed by tulle and silk.

My mother was a seemingly respectable woman, disdainful of her father's louche friends. Yet she herself had absorbed some of their worst qualities. She was an emotional tyrant, capricious as any fey ballerina, but without the redemptive grace of talent. She encouraged me to believe that she was the centre of my world, and I did believe it, at least when I was very small, fearing her tantrums as if they were the auguries of some terrible loss, an abandonment that would leave me out in the cold forever.

Ah, but my grandfather's *demi-monde* life was my refuge, with its aromas of passion, scandal, genius, sojourns in foreign countries. I loved it as much as I hated the suburban house in which I lived with my parents. I hated the television's fluttering blue glow, I hated the cries of children playing on their lawns at dusk while fireflies blundered in the uncertain light; I hated the smell of barbecues, the supermarkets and garage sales, the absence of style.

Given his half-Irish, half-Italian ancestry, I suppose my father should have been melodramatic, or dipsomaniacal. In fact he was a colourless man who worked in an office, too anxious for peace to protect me from my mother.

It is a November night in Manhattan; I am fourteen. My grandfather and I are having dinner in the Russian Tea Room. My grandfather eats very little, not because his appetite is small, but because he fears growing fat – he would feel marooned from himself if he let his slim dancer's body bloat into old age. He has an imperious head and large grey eyes. His name is Jacob. Although he is a Russian Jew, he prefers simply to say that he is Russian.

At fourteen I am too thin, with no qualms about eating blini and caviar. Grandfather is allowing me to drink a glass of vodka. I feel as though we are in a play:

> *Lily's uncle, the Count, has taken her to an opulent restaurant in St Petersburg, where they drink vodka and eat caviar served by waiters wearing Cossack tunics. Ladies and gentlemen bustle in, brush snow from their cloaks, bow to one another and cry, 'Good evening, Ivan Mikhailovich!' or 'Greetings, Natalia Sergeiovna!' Lily is preparing to 'come out', to lower her* décolletage, *put up her hair, and attend balls. Her uncle, the Count, is lecturing her on Society while she gazes demurely at her plate.*

What are we *really* talking about, in the Russian Tea Room on West 57th Street in Manhattan?

My grandfather is indeed lecturing me on Society. What he says is, 'You *can* get away, Lily, if you want to. You can live in Europe, where there is courtesy, culture – unlike this country where people make things up as they go along.'

I look at his determined mouth. 'How can I go away? We aren't rich. And you know my mother wouldn't let me.'

My grandfather's arm describes a crescent in the air; for an instant I see a ghostly scimitar. 'I will handle your mother. And you won't need money. Your youth is your wealth. As is your beauty.'

I know I am considered beautiful, more for my colouring than anything else. What astonishes people about my looks is that my hair is extraordinarily fair, of a hue fashion magazines call platinum or ash-blonde: silver rather than gold, closer to the moon than to the sun. But my 'doe-shaped' eyes are so dark a brown as to seem black, and I am told that against their darkness my hair shimmers and my skin is lustrous as pearls!

Yet I believe but for this accident of colouring I would not be beautiful. It could also be argued that my face is merely bizarre, that I am simply an anomaly since my kind of colouring is so rarely found in nature. As it is, my grandfather's theatrical friends caress my cheek and murmur praise in French or Russian. And my grandfather himself often gazes at me in his fierce, seagull-like way, and declares that my beauty will bring me fame and fortune. This prediction at once pleases and troubles me. It makes me feel yet again like a character in a play or an old-fashioned novel: the young heroine charged with promise, poised for romance. Yet a derisive voice in my head reminds me of my origins, the dull truth of my life, and assures me that I will never escape.

But, through my grandfather's connections, it was arranged for me to complete my education at a boarding school in England, at reduced fees. So I did get out, although, although . . .

At first I was exhilarated, an escaped convict, a refugee in reverse. Destiny had not been pitiless after all, had not consigned me for eternity to a bleak suburban life, to an unstable mother and an awkward father. And I had never liked America's hard landscape, so empty of history, while now, from my dormitory window, I could see moss-brocaded stone walls, ancient oaks, a Norman church, fields of gorse and hawthorn: such a deep landscape, even if it was not my own.

I was popular with the other girls because they considered me exotic, and I cultivated this perception, emphasising my Russianness just as my grandfather had done, and capitalising on my looks as he had instructed. And I was happy, moving among these girls who had been born into an old society, who lived in houses so ancient they bulged and sagged, who spoke in fluting English voices.

Still, the harsh New York accents of my father echoed in my head, as did the raucous voices of my Jewish relations as they argued politics across laden dining tables, slurping their soup, throwing up their hands in agitation. I pictured my hometown, which was really a kind of no-place, with its traffic lights depending from cords above the highways, its fast-food restaurants, despoiled landscape of gaunt trees and concrete playgrounds. I pictured those places, and was afraid my life in England was a lie in which I would be discovered, that I would be punished, banished from my own dreams, made to go back *there*, to that noisy prison.

At seventeen, I accompanied my school friend Vivian and her parents on their Christmas holiday to Nice. Vivian's father, a kindly painter, liked me in his vague way for my looks. 'Really, Lily,' he would suddenly exclaim, staring at me through his thick spectacles as though he had never seen me before, 'really, someone should paint you. You've got black eyes but your hair is pale as glass.' Only he never did paint me. He painted abstracts, solid-looking triangles and squares placed asymmetrically on immense canvases, which sold quite well. Vivian's serene mother was the editor of a woman's magazine.

December was balmy in Nice, the sky glossed with a marine radiance, the sea varying in colour from turquoise to lapis, the poplars and pewter olive trees vivid on the slopes. Because it wasn't hot, there were blessedly very few tourists.

In a haze of delight, Vivian and I wandered through *vieux* Nice, gazing at the sun-scoured houses painted gold or russet and scrolled over with wrought iron balconies. We stopped at cafés and marvelled at how different they were from English pubs, which struck us as somnolent compared to this bustle: the hiss and sputter of coffee machines, the deft movements of the waiters, the men at the *zinc* drinking pastis and talking heatedly. These men stared at us in candid admiration, their eyes limpid with sex. Unused to such scrutiny, we tried to laugh in a sophisticated way, feeling thrilled yet obscurely ashamed.

It was in Nice that I learned to love food. Vivian's parents were gourmets, but they loathed formal restaurants, which they considered pretentious and boring, so for our capacious evening meals we favoured the inexpensive *restaurants familial* that encircled our small hotel. These restaurants had names like La Petite Biche, or L'Aristocloche (because it was close to the basilica), or Le Restaurant Angleterre (because it was in the rue d'Angleterre, and also as a tribute to Nice's august history of tourists strolling along the Promenade des Anglais.) In them, I grew used to the flavours of the region: the pungency of niçoise olives, which are purple-black and small as currants; chunks of goat's cheese marinated in olive oil; salade niçoise dressed with that same strong oil; delicate fish like loup and dourade royale simply grilled and perfumed with fennel; daube de boeuf in a sauce rich as chocolate.

Vivian's father was never autocratic except in the restaurants, where he insisted that his daughter and myself overcome what he called our 'childish squeamishness' about dishes like calf's brains, veal kidneys, roast rabbit, tripe sausages, and steaks left blue in the middle. And after a period of nibbling gingerly at our food while he stared at us through ominously narrowed eyes, we did, finally, overcome our misgivings, enjoying everything he ordered for us and washing it all down with *pichets* of the local red wine – which, to our delight, Vivian's mother let us drink freely.

But it wasn't only food that I came to love in Nice; it was restaurants themselves, restaurants as a *phenomenon*, so to speak. I realised in France that restaurants are a kind of theatre; that each table is an oasis of privacy amid all the public clamour, that because of their peculiar intimacy (people confiding, confessing, laughing, quarrelling), restaurants are ideal for observing human nature, that they are, simply, exciting. One evening, the table across from our own was occupied by a beautiful couple – a woman with a lissom figure and sloe eyes and a man whose black skin had the violet lustre of aubergines. Throughout their meal, they caressed each other's faces; at one point the woman put her head in her hands and wept.

In another restaurant, there was always an old man eating alone. He was small and feeble and trembled the whole time, as though buffeted by an internal gale. Each night he took an elaborate meal, lifting his knife and fork in palsied hands, which shook so fiercely we were afraid that the food would tumble into his lap, yet he always managed to ferry each morsel into his mouth. He drank Campari from his own bottle which the plump waiter kept underneath the bar for him, and which he diluted with Perrier. And each night the proprietor would help him to the door and even onwards: an errand of mercy?

One evening, at one of our favourite restaurants, an elderly American couple occupied the table beside us. Glancing over, I recognised them as working-class New Yorkers; the man short and morose, with pouches beneath his lugubrious eyes, and the woman too plump and too bedizened, her hair coloured a vulgar orange, her arms festooned with bracelets. Something in me contracted with embarrassment and – yes – fear. *I am not like you, go away.*

All through that meal, they fascinated me. They had no table manners and found fault with everything. It was as though they were not in the South of France at all; they were so impervious to the society that surrounded them, and to the marvellous food. They could have been in their local deli, eating pastrami on rye and complaining about the world. 'What about Myrtle?' asked the woman at one point, 'Should I invite Myrtle?' This about some party they were intending to throw on their return to the States.

The man looked at her with his glum, extruding eyes. 'Nah. She's a cold fish.'

'When Bernie died she didn't go to the funeral.'

The man waved his hand contemptuously. 'That's what I told you. She's a cold fish.'

Cold fish? Were fish ever warm? And couldn't this sour man find any other metaphor?

When they had gone (after nibbling discontentedly at their dessert and showing no courtesy to the staff), I said to Vivian's father, 'Did you notice those sullen people beside us? They were so loud, and so ungracious to their waiter.'

'No,' he answered bemusedly, 'I didn't notice they were rude. I looked over at them once or twice. They seemed a nice old pair.'

I wasn't sure why, but I felt rebuked, somehow.

Another day, over aperitifs in the local café, while Vivian read a magazine and her parents discussed their painter friends, I took out my little diary and began to write about the restaurants; how they looked, what the proprietors and waiters were like, the food and wine. As I wrote, I became intensely aware of my surroundings. The usual suspects had collected in the café: the middle-aged lady who was forever at a table in the back, eating a salad while her dog slumbered at her feet; the bespectacled man consulting racing forms; the three men with caps and grizzled faces, like characters from *Fanny*; the sad-eyed blonde who drank glass after glass of pastis by herself.

'What are you writing?' asked Vivian's pleasant mother. When I showed her, her editor's eye narrowed appreciatively.

'Why, this is quite good, my dear. I could even put this in the magazine, in the travel section or perhaps the restaurant column.' She lowered the page and smiled at her husband. 'Really, this is awfully good, what Lily has done. It's almost a kind of new genre, a restaurant review that is *dramatic*, nearly a short story, so full of lavish descriptions and things. Yes, we could do something with this.'

And so began my career as a restaurant critic, first in London and then, after a few fits and starts, Dublin.

Part I

Dublin, 2000

Chapter I

Cliona's Restaurant
Dublin 2
by Lily Murphy

Tarnished Alice-in-Wonderland mirrors throw a silver light over the room. And there is a sombre glow from the immense bronze statue that stands beside the bar, of a boy with scalloped curls proffering a wine cup to the restaurant at large. Overall there is an impression of Edwardian opulence; one could imagine a portly merchant prince sauntering in amongst the orchids that decorate each table, accompanied by a lady with jewels in her hair. They would eat oysters and drink champagne, as a prelude to other matters, presumably.

So. This restaurant is camp, but not in an arch, snide

way – more in a funny way, with a relaxed staff who are amused by their customers. Moreover the food is relatively inexpensive, which could be another reason, in addition to its campness, that Cliona's attracts such an intriguing crowd: fewer captains of industry than one might expect, and more offbeat types. And the glowing room complements them. Three exquisitely dressed young men and one bedraggled man in jeans are eating mussels and talking seriously, their fingers gleaming with butter. At another table, a lone woman with hair flowing down to her hips is reading Dante's *Paradiso*. An illustrious Irish writer is drinking wine and speaking softly with a man who is probably his publisher. Three slightly tipsy elderly ladies are giggling in a corner, beneath one of the vast mirrors.

The food at Cliona's is pretty wonderful. There is a starter of spinach and lardons salad, which would be fairly ordinary but for the perfectly poached egg balanced on top, its white slightly pleated, like rumpled silk, its yolk the fault-less dome of the very fresh egg, until the fork pierces it and it flows lush and gold over the bright green spinach and chunks of bacon. The other starters are also good: home-made terrine of duck en croute; asparagus lightly cooked and topped with olive oil, red and black peppercorns and ragged leaves of parmesan; mussels done like escargots with garlic, parsley, and butter.

For the main course there is a delicious confit de canard, its skin delicate as puff pastry; a beautiful casserole of sweet-breads and mushrooms; excellent John Dory with an emul-sion of basil; and a few decent if unexciting pastas.

The desserts are uniformly splendid, and there is a generous plate of Irish farmhouse cheeses.

But the highlight of Cliona's is Cliona herself. A tall young woman with an almost Slavic face (high cheekbones and elongated eyes like two palm fronds), she has the ideal temperament for an owner-chef of a popular restaurant. Nothing flusters her! During one of our dinners, a lady across the room began to complain about her pasta. 'It's not properly *cooked*,' she shrilled. 'It's all *hard*.'

Despite the fact that the restaurant was thronged, Cliona herself hurried out of the kitchen, pushing back a tendril of hair that had come loose from her chignon. Her apron was covered in sauce, and there was a smudge of parsley on her cheek. But in a calm voice she explained to the lady that, at Cliona's, the spaghetti is cooked al dente, as the Italians do it.

'I don't *care* how foreigners do it,' cried the woman, her voice full of disdain for those Italian heathens who know nothing about how to cook pasta, 'I like my spaghetti properly *soft*.'

Unruffled, Cliona took the plate back into the kitchen, where another fresh one was prepared, probably boiled for about an hour according to the lady's wishes.

The simple fact is that this is a good restaurant because the food is way above average, and, despite the sumptuous room, the prices are below average. Plus it is unstuffy. And, incidentally, the wines are also decent and reasonably priced.

★

Lily's editor was a taut, shrewd woman whose style of dress reflected the attitudes of her magazine. *The Londoner*'s London was not a city of towers, steeples and parks; it was a city of shops and restaurants. And with her beautifully cut dresses and hair, her manicured hands and her expensive jewellery, Lily's editor looked perpetually like a prosperous lady who has just been shopping and is looking forward to lunch at a chic restaurant.

In January of 2000 she had called Lily into her office where, swivelling in her immense black chair before her immense and tidy desk, she had said, 'Don't ask me how it happened, but Ireland is *hot* these days.'

'So hot, it's cool?' murmured Lily.

'Exactly,' replied the editor, clearly unaware (as usual) of any irony in her protégé's comment, which was one of the things Lily liked, and also disliked, about her.

She went on, 'Dublin is full of money, which means full of restaurants, apparently some really *good* restaurants, although I don't suppose one has ever associated *Ireland* with good food.'

'Well, England doesn't have the world's best culinary reputation either,' the partly Irish Lily felt compelled to observe.

Her editor answered promptly, 'But England has had its mon-eyed classes for centuries, and the wealthy English have always eaten well: Dover sole, prawns, lamb and strawberries in season. Whereas Ireland is only just now coming into its own, economically speaking.' She put her elbows on the desk and narrowed her eyes. 'I'd like you to cover the restaurant scene in Ireland. I'd like you to move to Dublin, stay a while, a good long while, travel up and down, from Belfast to Cork to wherever, you know? How about it?'

Lily thought. She thought that she was getting a bit tired of London, which seemed to be growing ever more strident and pushy, like a version of New York. And she was also getting tired of the stubborn presence of Jacob and her mother in her imagination. She considered her diffident father, and how, through him, she was one-quarter Irish. She thought that she was lonely: she hadn't had a proper boyfriend in two years. She thought about Dublin across the sea: a sea change. 'Yes,' she said. 'Yes, I'd like to try Ireland.'

'Good, though you'd better be careful. They're a savage lot, the Irish.'

Lily regarded her equably. 'They managed to produce Yeats, and Joyce.'

'Oh, *Joyce*, with his incomprehensible books. I believe Virginia Woolf absolutely detested them.'

Lily genuinely couldn't tell if she was being teased. 'My name is Murphy, you know.'

'But you aren't *really* Irish, are you?' Twirling a pencil in her fingers, she seemed to reflect. 'In fact one doesn't know exactly *what* you are, my dear.' Then, with her tight smile, 'Which is, of course, part of your charm.'

In Dublin, Lily finally had her hair cropped short. For a long time she had been feeling oppressed by it, as though it were literally eclipsing her. She was thirty now, but over the years its colour had neither dimmed nor darkened, and when she walked along the street with that silver banner flowing down her back, attracting all kinds of attention – well, it had begun to be a drag. When she realised that certain colleagues were referring to her as 'the one with the hair', she'd begun to see that it was time to do something about it.

'Short, please,' she'd told the hairdresser, looking steadily at him in the mirror. She had felt uncomfortable in the salon because it was so like a hospital, full of docile women in blue gowns being ferried from washbasin to chair, where the professional waited, smiling consolingly before his array of instruments.

'Right,' he had said, his bluntness complementing her own, narrowing his eyes to ponder her head, refraining from banal talk about the weather, just getting to work, asking her to tilt forward so that she could feel the cold touch of his scissors on her nape.

'I've released the wave,' he announced with satisfaction when it was over. 'I bet you thought your hair was straight? It was only that it was so heavy, it hadn't a chance to curl.'

Now, a day later, surveying herself in the mirror, Lily still was not sure how she felt. Her hair had been transformed into a welter of loose waves. She stared and stared, feeling, as always, uneasy about her so-called beauty, nearly certain it was just a trick of colouring, of light and shadow. Sometimes she thought this was the truth of all her life, that it was a trick, a lie, a dream. She had done this before, had stood before the mirror in silent communion with herself, asking her image that adolescent question, but asking it with real perplexity: *Who am I?*

She roused herself, and hurriedly put on a jacket, since it was an unusually cold April evening. She was going to dinner for her column, going alone, since she had not yet made friends in Dublin.

At the table, she swept off her beret, shook out her new curls, and lowered her head to contemplate the menu, deliberately meeting no one's eye since dining alone was problematic – for a woman. Lunch was all right; you could be an office worker gobbling a meal between appointments. But people still considered a woman having dinner on her own in a fashionable restaurant either mysterious or pitiable. Sometimes Lily liked it, the speculation that would encircle her, the quick glances from neighbouring tables, while she ate her solitary supper. But tonight she was feeling shy, perhaps because Dublin was new to her. The waiter appeared, and she ordered avocado and prawns, grilled salmon with fennel and a half-bottle of Macon Villages. It was an extensive menu; she would have to come here again.

After the starter, she surreptitiously took out her little book and scribbled, *Avocado just right, prawns fresh but slightly overcooked, sauce okay.* Then she glanced round to make certain no one was observing her; it would not do for the staff to register that she was a restaurant critic, especially since she was as yet unknown in Dublin, whereas in London she had been forced, after a time, to concoct absurd disguises – dark glasses, floppy hats – coy as a film star.

With a small shock she noticed that the man beside her was also writing in a little book. Like herself he was eating alone, but there was a whole bottle of wine on his table as opposed to her modest half. She studied him furtively. He was about fifty-five, she thought, and over-elegant in the way of slight men who dress too fastidiously and impress you as fussy rather than dapper. A popinjay. And his narrow face and tapering beard gave him the look of a wolf. At the moment she observed this, he met her eye and threw her a lupine grin.

'Reviewing, are we?' he asked, still smiling in a teeth-baring way.

'Hush,' she answered brusquely, 'please don't blow my cover.'

'I would never do such an ungallant thing. May I come to your table, dear lady?' Without waiting for a reply he seized his wine bottle and moved to the chair across from her own. She nearly protested – before noticing that he was drinking an extremely rare Burgundy, way beyond her wine budget. *You unscrupulous minx,* she said to herself, *You are going to let him stay because you want a glass of that La Tache!*

The man extended his right hand and 'Count Bartholomew O'Sullivan-Kelly,' he announced, with another glinting smile.

'Er – hello. I'm Lily.'

'A-ha! I knew it. Lily Murphy, restaurant connoisseur and critic for *The Londoner*. I have seen your face in photographs. May I help myself to a soupcon of your delightful Macon Villages? Then we can call for another white, before savouring the *piece de resistance*, this absolutely splendid La Tache. Anyway, dear girl, what *are* you doing in Dublin?'

Disconcerted by this man's deft patter, and by the impertinence with which it was so liberally seasoned, Lily answered confusedly, 'I'm living here now. I mean, the magazine has asked me to be its restaurant correspondent in Ireland.'

'A-ha!' Count O'Sullivan-Kelly repeated. 'Then you are both colleague and rival to myself. You see, I, too, am a restaurant critic, for *Emerald Isle*, an appalling name for a magazine, you would doubtless agree, with its mawkish American associations.

Shamrocks and leprechauns! However, it pays rather handsomely.'

'So I've noticed.' She indicated his bottle. '*The Londoner* would never allow me to drink such a good wine.'

'But your Macon Villages is quite nice, although it seems we have polished it off. Shall we try a half bottle of Chablis, while we wait for the main course?'

Lily murmured assent; she was not quite sure why, since the wine she had already drunk was going a little to her head. But for some reason she was warming to this curious man with his baroque name and flamboyant diction, deciding, in a wine-flushed way, that he was rather amusing after all, rather interesting, and, of course, as he himself had observed, a colleague. Probably it was only the drink inclining her to be expansive, along with her current loneliness, but she was suddenly ready to befriend him. And also ready, for some reason she did not want to analyse, to get a bit drunk.

The Count was saying, 'I must tell you why gustatory journalism is my profession. I am a younger son, you see. My brother was given a purpose in life upon his birth, but I have had to make my own way in the world. And very early on, I realised that I loved a good table.'

The waiter came with their half bottle of Chablis. O'Sullivan-Kelly continued, 'We grew up in a grand yet slightly *mouldering* house, and the kitchen was a disgrace. Even as a child, my heart grew heavy at mealtimes. The dining room was cold as a tomb, the conversation exclusively about horses, yet all that I could have borne, had there been any comfort in the plates put before me by our gloomy butler. But it was terrible, dear girl, terrible! Shoe-leather meat, watery vegetables, puddings that resembled the plump and unhealthy face of my nanny. Unendurable!'

Their main courses arrived. Lily examined her salmon, which was nicely crusty from the grill, then took a nibble of it, feeling self-conscious in the presence of another restaurant critic. The Count, she observed through her lashes, was doing the same, scrutinising his magret de canard then trying a piece, all the while throwing her covert glances. They both paused in their eating to scribble furiously in their books.

'May I try yours?' she asked. 'It looks very nice. Would you like a bit of mine?' She was uncomfortably aware that her offer sounded more suggestive than she had intended, but language about food is always fraught, if you weren't careful, and it was hard to be careful while drinking such a strong wine.

She studied him while he savoured a morsel of her salmon, wondering if he thought it good. His duck was delicious, rosy in the middle and tender. They both munched concentratedly, neither of them volunteering an opinion. Rivals indeed, she thought with amusement, we are both playing our cards close to the chest – or breast of duck, in this instance. The Count poured her another glass of La Tache, and resumed his story.

'So, Miss Murphy. That is my history, in a *coquille de noix*, the reason I am here with you now, concentrating all my critical abilities on my palate. Incidentally,' he said suddenly, as if deciding at last to favour her with a culinary opinion, 'our broccoli is rather undercooked, isn't it? I mean, we all like a bit of crunch, but this is practically *raw*.'

Lily was too puzzled to reply. She had never met such a creature before, and it struck her that he was like a P. G. Wodehouse character.

The Count declared that she must call him Bartholomew, and

insisted that they drink a half bottle of claret with the cheese, so that by the time they left the restaurant Lily was feeling pretty drunk. The sky seemed to sway and her legs were wobbling slightly. She inhaled the cool night air, and felt better. The street was nearly empty. She wondered if Bartholomew was gay, and if he was straight, if he would try to kiss her, but he merely brought her hand to his lips with the archaic courtesy that seemed natural to him, and murmured, 'We shall doubtless meet again, dear girl.'

Walking blearily along Baggot Street to her room at the Arts Club, Lily observed that her responses to the Count were complicated. She was certainly relieved he hadn't tried to kiss her, since she wasn't attracted to him despite finding him urbane and amusing. Yes, all in all, she was glad that he had taken his leave of her so graciously, without trying to entice her into further intimacies.

And yet . . . she had to acknowledge that she was vaguely disappointed. In her drunken and vulnerable state, the thought of a man, any man, drawing her close in an embrace, brushing his mouth against her cheek, her lips – she had to admit this thought was exciting, and that it quickened a loneliness in her which was too deep.

She trudged up to her room, avoiding the thronged bar, and forced herself to drink a large glass of water. Then she collapsed into bed. But sleep wouldn't come.

She was thinking about the last man she had really known, her last boyfriend, called Hugo Cross. He was film critic for *The Londoner*, a good critic, if sometimes too lacerating when describing movies he considered to be bad. He was three years her senior, and far more self-possessed in the world than she. She had met him when she was twenty-four, and they had parted two years ago, at around the time of her twenty-eighth birthday.

To some degree, she had loved Hugo because he was formal, because he had emerged from the kind of background where form is placed naturally upon life. Lily had so disliked the dishevelled nature of her own early years, the haphazard meals, the absence of ceremony. One of the reasons she loved restaurants, with their fuss and decorum, was that she had always yearned for *style*, whether the bohemian style of her grandfather, or the more traditional English upper middle-class style of her boarding school and, of course, of Hugo.

Things had begun to go wrong between them for a reason she was ashamed of, because she feared that it would reveal her as gauche and childish. It was simply that he was a terrible flirt, and his flirtatiousness ignited a wild insecurity in her. She had not actually doubted Hugo's constancy, for after this party or that, where he would have engaged in a smouldering flirtation with any number of women, he always went home with her and no one else.

Still, his flirting inflicted a dread and an anguish on her, and she soon realised it was the women she feared; not Hugo, but the women whom he encouraged with his caressing looks, his banter, his clasping of their hands. Lily feared that the world was peopled with cruel women whose rapacity would expose her to Hugo as the charlatan she was. She feared his attentions flooded the veins of these women with a kind of power, that because he admired a girl at some party she was able to look at Lily and say triumphantly, *I know who you really are, you cannot deceive me!* Yes, she feared women, feared their coquetry, their guile; feared they were powerful, and that under their appraising eyes she was powerless. But did she *truly* believe that other women could somehow divine her secrets, humiliate her and take Hugo from her? Hugo, whom she cherished but did not deserve?

She did not know if she was really convinced, on her deepest level, that the world was thronged with gloating sirens; she did not know much beyond her feelings of helplessness and fury. But she would have liked to tell Hugo that it was not enough for him to go home with her and make love to her after he had ignored her all evening at a drinks party or a gallery opening. She had wanted to tell him he should acknowledge his affection for her in company as well as in private, that such acknowledgement was merely the social – the public – face of love.

But she never told him, because she was afraid he would accuse her of mean jealousy. She had imagined his fine eyes darkening with annoyance, and his crisp English voice rebuking her for trying to control him, that he was surprised at how silly she could be, that he was *disappointed* in her. She had imagined this, and had kept silent.

And her silence had destroyed them. Her fear, unspoken, congealed into a kind of cynicism, as though she had indeed become convinced the world was full of betrayal and sorrow. Alarmed by how vulnerable love had made her, and afraid of rejection, of exposure, she had withdrawn from Hugo. She withdrew into her work, bringing him, still, to the restaurants with her, but barely attending to him, concentrating instead on this dish or that sauce, talking only about the service, the décor, the salad dressing. At first he had been patient, though perplexed, no doubt, by what he must have thought was a new coldness in her. But she never cleared up the mystery, never confided in him until, exasperated by her remoteness, her unresponsiveness, the disappearance of her ardour in bed, he left her.

Now here she was, thirty years old, in her billet at the Dublin City Arts Club, deeply lonely, still afraid of life, still practising concealment. The only real love affair she'd ever had was with some myth of herself, which she had created out of fear and which she was still sustaining. Over the years her American accent had softened towards an English one, and, with her platinum hair and black eyes, no one could be certain of her origins. Her life, in other words, was to some extent a disguise, but she could not expunge the Lily whom she used to be, and in her inmost self she was hungry for love.

Suddenly, she got up out of bed, splashed water on her face, and struggled back into her clothes. She was still faintly drunk, but since sleep was eluding her and her unbidden thoughts were so unpleasant, she decided she would descend into the bar, which she could tell was still lively. She could dimly hear laughter, and the gurgle of drinks being poured. Why not? she thought, Why not have a drink with the *habitués* of this curious club, since I won't sleep anyway?

It was well after midnight, but obviously the Dublin City Arts Club (affectionately known as the DC/AC) disdained such boring technicalities as having a closing time. Pausing in the doorway, Lily registered that some people were still ebulliently tipsy, drinking pints and laughing, while others had grown drowsy and were slumping at the bar.

The room was plain, just a number of chairs, sofas and low

tables, nearly all of them occupied. When she walked in, heads swivelled to regard her, but she didn't feel shy, since the curiosity amongst these people seemed benign. Besides, it was clear that their main passion was drink, at this hour anyway, and that their interest in a newcomer would not extend beyond a vague friendliness. She would be safe here, but, as with Bartholomew earlier, the knowledge of such safety was obscurely disappointing.

She recognised some faces; after all, she'd been living in the place for nearly three weeks, and had naturally noticed a few regulars, though this was the first time she had actually ventured into the bar. The regular who was most familiar to her, a bearded man with a kindly face, was speaking to another, elderly man who was handsome in a brittle way, with that delicate, almost friable skin so ubiquitous among the Irish. This man looked rather dashing, with a black scarf thrown over one shoulder, and the lamplight gleaming on his silver hair. In the far corner, a singing session had just begun, launched by a beautiful girl with profuse black curls, along with an older woman in a pink blouse.

Lily settled at the bar beside a solitary man who was smoking a French cigarette. He seemed younger than most of the others in this room, closer in age to herself and to the lovely black-haired girl, perhaps forty or so. She gave him a quick glance, which told her that his face was slender and handsome, and that he had longish, rather floppy dark hair. The fingers holding the French cigarette were unusually long. He did not intercept her glance because he was frowning into the glass of whiskey before him on the bar.

Resisting the desire to take drink, she called for a mineral water. Behind her, the old lady wearing pink was clasping her hands in a beatific way, and warbling the first stanzas of 'She Moved Through the Fair'. The man beside Lily said, 'You're new here.'

She turned to look at him, but once again he did not meet her eyes, this time because he was concentrating on lighting another cigarette. His expression was laconic, almost guarded. She sensed that this was his habitual mien, a kind of rueful look, somewhere between a smile and a frown. In fact, his mouth was bracketed with lines, and she reflected he might be older than she had thought. She said, 'Yes. And I am new to Dublin, as well.'

Still not looking at her, he observed, 'You're not the usual Arts Club type.'

'What *is* the usual Arts Club type?'

Finally, he regarded her. His smile deepened. 'Older. Rather good people on the whole, though there are some bastards. They love drink, and they're pretty eccentric, which is nice. But very few of them are artists.'

'Please tell me about them.'

'Some of them are institutions, like that man with the yellow waistcoat. His name is Malachy O'Malley and he is a sort of professional Man About Town. Quite witty, which I suppose would be a requirement for a Man About Town. The large man with red hair and red trousers is famous for insulting his friends, but he's very popular. Have you ever noticed how certain people enjoy being abused? Well, all kinds of people swarm to this man's house where he serves them brandy in dirty teacups and humiliates them. Yet they feel privileged, and tell him what a genius he is. The woman who is singing owns a second-hand bookshop. The girl beside her is her niece. She's half Jewish' (Lily felt a faint shock of apprehension) 'which may explain those exotic curls' (she sighed with relief).

He went on, 'That woman with the halo of grey hair is a

famous Communist, and the man she is lecturing is called The Fecker O'Reilly. He needs the lecture, because he's an arrogant old fecker, hence the name. The small man who looks as if he was moulded from wood is Hugh de Blackpoole, but everyone calls him Horrible Hugh. He's a Papal Count. Extremely stupid, though harmless enough.'

Lily said, 'Speaking of Counts, do you know one called O'Sullivan-Kelly?'

He laughed, his eyes crinkling; they were smallish, and lovely for their colour, grey with glints of blue – like the sea in autumn, Lily thought. All his lines were long and supple, the kind of body that relaxes naturally into an elegant slouch. 'The restaurant man? I have seen him about. He's something of a crackpot, from a family of crackpots, they say.'

'*She came in so softly, her feet made no din,*' sang the elderly lady in her unsteady voice; she had launched into the song for the second time. Lily said to the man beside her, 'Clearly you are not a typical Arts Club member either.'

He laughed again. 'I come here because they serve drink nearly all night. I finish my work late, when the pubs are closed.' He paused to light another cigarette. Then, 'I am a chef,' he said.

Lily also laughed, and when he looked quizzically at her she exclaimed, 'I can't escape the world of food! You're a chef, and I am a restaurant critic, like that man O'Sullivan-Kelly, who waylaid me at my dinner tonight.' She introduced herself, and told him about her column in *The Londoner*, and how her editor had assigned her to cover Ireland, since by all accounts its restaurant scene was flourishing.

He gave his wry smile. 'Yeah, flourishing. Which can be an

appalling drag. The food world is so pretentious, and it shouldn't *matter* so much.'

She knew what he meant. When a society was flush with money, as Ireland had suddenly become (at least in certain quarters), an effete passion for wine and food often began to take over. At times she was faintly disgusted by her own columns, the solemn descriptions of this kind of mushroom or that kind of Brussels sprout, the lofty assertions that wild salmon is superior to farmed, raw milk cheeses to pasteurised, ignoring the fact that many people may not be able to afford chanterelles or salmon or fine fromages.

'It's awful how foodies *diminish* things,' she said in agreement. 'They journey to a village in the south of France or a city in Italy, and afterwards they talk about nothing but some plate of mussels or bottle of wine they had there.'

He looked at her with another brief smile. 'Yet here we are, the pair of us, working in that world.'

Something about his smile unsettled her. It was nearly sardonic, and those grey eyes with their blue sheen seemed to be taking her measure. He did not strike her as unkind, only extremely alert, with the kind of ironic intelligence that does not suffer fools gladly.

He wrote something on a drinks napkin, and pushed it across to her. She read 'Restaurant Matisse' and an address in central Dublin.

He finished his drink and stood, extending his hand. 'Please come for dinner one night, when you are *off duty*.'

It was only after he had left that she realised she didn't know his name.

Chapter II

Farfalle
Dublin 4
by Lily Murphy

There was a time when you could recognise a cheap Italian restaurant by its red and white tablecloths and candles burning in Chianti bottles, or an expensive French by its rosy lamplight and embellished mirrors. In other words, restaurants used to convey a sense of their national cuisine through a series of pleasant, decorative clichés. Now, however, most restaurants just look like restaurants, and one wouldn't know, walking into this or that stylish place, whether it served up sushi or steak tartare.

That is why I gave a silent groan when I first entered this arid room. I am sure that the proprietors of Farfalle believe that their décor is highly innovative, but to my eye the place looks exactly like those immense, severely appointed restaurants that erupted all over London in the 1980s. There are the same grey walls decorated with grey abstract paintings, the same extra-long bar, and enough tables to create a fearsome din when the place is full. All very austere and self-conscious, and all wearily familiar.

Yet the clientele do not seem to know, or care, that this restaurant is not as boldly cool as it obviously thinks it is. They throng the place – young, glossy with money, bellowing into their mobile phones – gluttons of consumerism. But they, like the restaurant, are not as cool as they think. Yuppies were a 1980s phenomenon, and it is nearly eerie to see them resurrected here, just as confident as the baby bankers of London or New York twenty years ago. And, also like their predecessors, they seem curiously without discernment, despite their new, aggressive prosperity. It seems clear that style, or anyway what they perceive as style, means more to them than substance.

For the food here is really bad. Let me say, before I continue, that I have always loved those Italian starters which are not cooked but merely 'composed', in contrast to a friend of mine who adores elaborate cookery and who once complained, 'I hate it when one goes to some Italian place and they arrange bits of cheese and vegetables on a plate, pour oil on top, and serve it up as if it were a proper *cooked* dish.' But surely this is the essence of good Italian food, pure ingredients presented simply. Insalata caprese, for example, when it's made with the kind of buffalo mozzarella that shines like satin on the outside and is almost creamy inside, and comes dressed with fresh basil and ripe tomatoes and lashings of olive oil. Or a plate of air-cured beef and olives, or prosciutto and figs, or a salad of rocket and parmesan, et cetera. It isn't as easy as it seems, for the flavours must be properly balanced, and of course the ingredients must be absolutely fresh and fine.

Which brings me back to the appalling Farfalle. The starter of Parma ham has the texture of wood and the flavour of nothing, the mozzarella and tomato salad consists of anaemic tomatoes and rubbery cheese drenched in cheap olive oil, and the antipasti are full of those disgusting, synthetic olives that come out of bottles.

There is one good pasta, of linguine in truffle oil with wild mushrooms, but the other three on the menu are mediocre and over-priced. As for the main courses, the osso buco manages to be at once dry and greasy, and the roast salmon offered as the fish of the evening had been cooked to death. There is a lovely plate of gorgonzola and pears, or else an array of insipid puddings. The wines are insultingly expensive.

I suppose that I feel such ire about this restaurant because in every provincial Italian town (less so these days in the big cities) you can still eat a superb meal in an unpretentious restaurant for very little money. You can settle at a plain table and be served local wine in a brown pitcher, a plate of home-made pasta, some fresh veal or fish, and good cheese with good bread and olives, all for the price of one of the unfortunate starters at Farfalle. The young waiters and waitresses are gracious enough, but there is a sort of manager, a tall man with a grim mouth, who fastens a baleful eye on them and berates them publicly for the smallest error, which of course flusters them into making more mistakes. All in all, an unpleasant experience.

★

'You are a pitiless girl,' said a voice on the phone.

She had been looking out of her window, at the slender Georgian houses opposite, and thinking that in some ways Dublin was a perfect city, all washed sky and fine stone, encircled by mountains and the sea. The night before she had walked home through Trinity College, its cobbles silvered with moonlight and a smell of brine on the wind. And this morning the sky was full of gulls, their cries making her feel she was on a ship, she and the whole of Dublin scudding along beneath those windblown clouds.

'Who *is* this?' she asked.

'I failed to introduce myself, the other night. My name is Nicholas Savage.'

'That sounds a pitiless name.'

'Well, savage I may be, but I don't go about bashing nice people's restaurants.'

'You mean the Farfalle review? I am not supposed to consider a proprietor's niceness, I am supposed to serve up the culinary truth, for my loyal readers. That place is dreadful. The food was terrible except for the blue cheese and pears thing at the end, and the manager is a brute. I saw him hector a barmaid until she cried.'

There was a silence. Then, 'Would you like to go on a drive with me, into the Wicklow mountains?'

He arrived at midday, driving a small red car. She had put on a black jersey and black jeans, and was relieved to observe he was also casually dressed, though more colourfully than herself, in a green jumper and saffron-coloured trousers – he had offered to take her to lunch at a country restaurant that he liked, only she had neglected to ask him if it was formal.

She felt shy, climbing in beside him, and wondered if it was always like this, whether one was fifteen or fifty, that warm tumult of anticipation beforehand, and then the sudden, stiff shyness at the moment of meeting.

Driving south, he said, 'I didn't want to wait for you to come to the restaurant. I wanted to see you sooner, especially after reading your column, which I found amusing.'

As in the Arts Club bar, he did not look at her while he spoke, as though he were addressing the Stillorgan dual carriageway. In a voice low with shyness she answered, 'I was pleased when you rang. And I have never been to Wicklow.'

The sky glowed with that deep light she had come to recognise as peculiarly Irish, an interior radiance, as though the clouds were exhaling it. All around them the air shone pale gold, while a deeper gold flared on the mountains in the distance, which looked to Lily like sleeping animals, with their rough brown hides. This landscape fascinated her because it seemed at once sere and lush, all tough grass and heather, with bunches of gorse making sunbursts of colour against the rocks.

They wound higher and higher into the mountains, barely speaking. She was still feeling tense and shy, and supposed that he was, too. Presently they stopped in Roundwood.

'They've made it look Alpine,' said Nicholas, 'with those black-and-white pubs. I suppose they feel an affinity with the Tyrol, because the village is so high up, but it's a bit disconcerting. I keep expecting to see people in lederhosen. Would you like an aperitif?'

He brought her into a large whitewashed pub, whose facade did look Tyrolean, although the inside was utterly Irish, with the customers, mostly men, gazing into their pints and talking in low, stout-blurred voices. A group of young men and women were clustered at a table before the empty fireplace, drinking bottles of cider and laughing. The barman was slight, with a furrowed face and startlingly abundant hair that surged back from his brow in one grey mass.

'Afternoon, Nick,' he said with solemn courtesy, smiling gravely at Lily also. He was moving a cloth over the counter in an exaggeratedly precise way, which made her conclude he was a bit drunk, or anyway at that point of inebriation when people sometimes become extremely earnest and concentrated, as if to emulate sobriety. Nicholas introduced him as Eugene Byrne, 'a real Wicklow man and a fine publican.'

They settled at the counter, and Nicholas surprised her by calling for champagne. Champagne in a country pub? But the bottle Eugene Byrne produced from underneath the bar was actually quite good, which encouraged her to think there was something singularly charming, perhaps even slightly enchanted, about this journey into the mountains.

In the restaurant – a pleasantly rustic place with two ample rooms, the tables made of dark wood – she said, 'I liked that man, Eugene Byrne.'

'He liked you as well, or he wouldn't have offered us that special bottle. Sometimes, late at night, he hears fairy orchestras playing outside in the fields, or sees fairy women combing their long hair in the moonlight. I imagine we would see fairies too, if we hadn't drawn a sober breath in twenty years.' Nicholas was frowning at the menu. 'Do you like gravlax? They do it here with a homemade mayonnaise, full of mustard and dill. And then I'd recommend the lamb, great Wicklow lamb, though they'll overcook it unless you tell them not to.'

He called for a Pouilly-Fumé. Sunlight, flowing in through the open windows, struck their glasses and deepened the wine's hue to honey. Lily drank slowly. She was terrifically hungry, and the leaves of gravlax, coral-coloured, pungent against the rich sauce, were delicious.

He asked her about her background, and of course she paused, gazing at her plate of roast lamb and roast parsnips, the red wine in both their glasses.

'I am originally from America,' she said carefully, 'but I never felt at home there. My mother's people are Russian; my grandfather was a dancer in the New York City ballet. When my parents sent me to school in England, I knew I'd found my home on this side of the Atlantic, a bit like a latter-day Henry James, I suppose. My parents have flown over to visit me now and again, not too often, which suits me well enough, since I wasn't particularly happy as a child, and so I can't say I yearn to see them all that much.' She paused, hoping he would not question her more closely.

What he said was, 'Such an exotic history. Your accent is not at all American.'

Hurriedly she asked, 'And you? Where do you come from?'

It was clear to her that he was also suddenly slightly uncomfortable, staring downwards, fussily arranging the meat and vegetables into a pattern on his plate. 'Belfast,' he mumbled.

'Why, you have no Northern accent.'

'I jettisoned it as soon as I learnt to speak properly. It's harsh and mean, like the place itself.'

The wine had relaxed her into uttering a thought she might ordinarily have kept to herself: 'You were not – at ease – in the place that was your first home. Like me.'

He glanced up with a small smile. 'We are, perhaps, similar in that way, even though we are so different.'

So he was also ashamed. Ashamed of Belfast? Was he Catholic or Protestant? And did he come from one of those beleaguered housing estates, or perhaps a more middle-class area, where he would have learnt about good cooking from prosperous parents? Well, she was not about to ask, or not yet anyway.

Nicholas distracted her by asking if she would like coffee. He was still smiling. It occurred to her that some important signal had just passed between them. *We are, perhaps, similar in that way.* And while they lingered over coffee she began to anticipate the journey home. She was registering that his work had made him strong: a forearm, emerging from the bunched sleeve of his jersey and resting on the table, was taut and corded, and his shoulders were very broad. For some reason her eyes clung to the hollow between his collarbones, as though drawn to that ordinary place by some fairy spell. Suddenly his fingers brushed her hand across the table, the first time he had touched her.

'We should go,' he said softly. 'Let's go.'

But as they rose, a vaguely familiar voice cried from behind, 'Dear girl, is it really you? I can scarcely believe it!'

They turned to regard Bartholomew O'Sullivan-Kelly, flushed and smiling above his arrow of a beard, elegantly *sportif* in tweeds, extending a hand to each of them.

The courtesies were exchanged, after which the Count chortled, 'It is perfect timing that I should meet you here. My dear friend Theo Herbert – he is, you know, descended from Lord Ballsbridge – is at this moment having a little drinks party at his house which is quite nearby, and he is a great admirer of Mr Savage's restaurant, *and* he would be delighted to make *your* acquaintance, I am sure of it, dear lady. You *must* stop with me there, immediately, if only for a quick libation.'

Helpless before his firmness, they followed him out into the road.

They drove along an avenue of trees, their boughs interlacing overhead to create a bosky tunnel splashed here and there with sunlight. Then a medieval-looking gate swung magically open before Bartholomew's car, and they continued down a broad drive. The house appeared suddenly, like Manderley. It was all pink stone, large windows warm with early evening light and sweeping lawns.

'Who will be inside that house?' Lily speculated.

Nicholas, gliding up beside the Count's car, said with a laugh, 'I suppose you've never seen the local aristocracy at play? You're in for an experience, I'd imagine.'

The Count gestured them into a drawing room dominated by a vast painting above the mantel. Gazing at it, Lily received an impression of abundant, peachy flesh. Gradually she realised it portrayed some kind of divine rape: an immense god, eyes bulging (and with another bulge clearly visible beneath his blue loincloth), was bearing down on a nymph or maiden who lay naked on the black loam at his feet, her arms flung wide.

'Awful, isn't it?' said a dry female voice.

Lily turned, startled; she had thought the room unoccupied. But a thin woman was reclining on a red sofa, a cigarette in her fingers. She was wearing a sleeveless scarlet dress, and Lily noticed that her arms were white as milk against the bright fabric. She had a sharp pretty face, and very short black hair.

'Why, *Nicholas*,' she cried the very next moment, swinging her legs to the floor and rising in one feline motion, 'How marvellous to see *you* here.'

She extended a hand, laughing, and Nicholas bowed over it, with one of his ironical smiles.

Immediately Lily's heart fell. She could smell a coquette a mile away, and her reaction was always the same: her arms and legs literally stiffening with dismay. It was as though all the warm talk she had exchanged with Nicholas that day had at this moment come to ashes. She barely knew him, yet she was prepared, now, to stop seeing him completely, merely because another woman was smiling into his face and talking gaily to him. It was always the same; whenever a girl flirted with a man Lily liked, she felt that premonition of loss – not only of someone dear to her but the loss, somehow, of herself. And while she suspected that this feeling was not actually a premonition but an echo, a shadow, of some sorrow from her past, still the hurt and fear remained. This stranger was upper class, self-assured, lissom in her red dress (the same vivid red as her lips – and the sofa from which she had risen). Beside her, Lily felt an utter fake: *Who am I?*

The woman placed cool fingers on Lily's hand. 'I am Sylvie. *Isn't* the picture terrible? I don't know where Ballsy got it from, or why he has put it up there so that everybody is *obliged* to stare all day long at those sub-Rubens creatures. The girl looks massive enough to resist that fellow in the loincloth, doesn't she? She's prob-ably only *pretending* to be upset, and then when he's off his guard she'll *pummel* him.'

Bartholomew said querulously, 'Sylvie, where is everyone? I brought these people here for a party.'

She waved her cigarette in the air. 'Don't know where the staff are. Probably down in the cellar, guzzling the Master's claret. Ballsy is giving the others a tour of the grounds.'

Just then, as if, Lily thought, they were all characters in a play, a French door opened, and a tall man sauntered in, followed by another man and a woman. The first man, apparently Theo Herbert, was rather brutally handsome, with an almost thuggish curl to the lip, and heavy eyes. He must have been a sullen dark boy, Lily said to herself, while all his family were fair and light-hearted; so he felt like a changeling among them and now he sulks deliber-ately and emphasises his differentness. The second man, in con-trast, was florid, blond and plump. Both he and Herbert were in their early fifties, she decided, but the woman accompanying them looked considerably younger, about the age of Sylvie, slightly older than Lily herself. She had a pleasant sallow face and straight sallow hair that swung over her shoulders when she moved. Herbert and his rubicund friend were wearing suits, but she was dressed casually, in jeans and a grey jumper.

Bartholomew made the introductions, and when Herbert clasped Lily's hand, staring at her from beneath the black hair that flowed across his brow, she felt a slight shock at the force of his curious, saturnine power. His smile bordered on a sneer, but when he spoke it was to say cordially, 'Welcome to my house. I do so enjoy your delightful articles.' According to the Count, his name was Theodore; everyone called him Theo, except Sylvie, of course, whose cheeky diminutive for him he seemed not to mind. The man with the ruddy face was introduced as Christopher, and the woman with the pleasant smile as Philippa.

Everyone arranged themselves on the chairs and sofas, Nicholas settling beside Lily on a brocade couch. She was still completely ignorant of the relationships among these people; they could have been husbands and wives, brothers and sisters, friends or strangers. Magically, or again as if they were all in a play, a butler appeared, bearing a magnum of champagne, which he poured into thin flutes that shone silver in the dusky light. He handed them round, then moved swiftly from table to table, turning on the lamps, before vanishing as soundlessly as he had come.

In an English accent, the man called Christopher said, 'Splendid what you've done here, Theo. In England, all the finest lands are being chopped up by the Jews and made into housing estates – or concentration camps! – for the hoi polloi.' He gave a shout of laughter.

Theo, lounging on a sofa, gave this Christopher his surly stare. But he did not speak. Lily felt her face grow warm. The ugliness of the man – his face blunt and stupid as a fist, those porcine eyes – and the ugliness of his words, were making her tremble. Yet she, also, did not speak.

It was Sylvie who cried, 'Oh, don't talk such absolute *rot* about the Jews, Christopher. You sound like those National Front fools who say the Holocaust never happened.'

'I have it on sound authority that it *did* never happen,' Christopher replied blandly, 'and the National Front are not fools, you silly girl. They are merely trying to protect the purity of the English race. And if you ask me, Ireland ought to consider becoming a bit more vigilant in that regard as well, since all these immigrants have been pouring in – immigrants and Jews.'

Suddenly, Nicholas said in a low voice, 'Careful.'

'What was that, dear boy?' Christopher's marble eyes turned towards Nicholas, who was drawing deeply on one of his French cigarettes.

'I said be careful. You know, Savage is a Jewish name.'

Christopher turned red as a beefsteak. Lily saw Theo smile. Nicholas clasped her hand on the couch.

Philippa, the hazel-haired girl, put her glass abruptly down on the carpet and cried, 'I am *desperately* tired. And if I drink any more champagne I shall fall asleep right here. I'll give you a lift into town, Christopher, if you promise not to talk any more racist rubbish.'

Everybody stood up. Sylvie moved close to Lily and touched her hand again. 'You are so beautiful,' she said kindly, 'but we haven't had a chance to speak. Perhaps you would like to meet in Dublin one day, for a coffee or a drink?'

Lily smiled gratefully. She still couldn't really believe in her beauty, but who would object to being called lovely, and by a woman whom she had so obviously misjudged?

She said, 'Maybe you would like to have dinner with me, for one of my reviews? If you wouldn't mind being a guinea pig!'

'I certainly wouldn't mind being fed truffles. That would be splendid.'

They moved outside. Night had fallen, and the air smelled of earth and leaves. Suddenly a light came on, illuminating the silent lawn, already spangled with dew. After good-byes, everyone but Lily, Nicholas and the Count moved to the back of the house, where their cars were. Bartholomew, meanwhile, bowed over Lily's hand and said, 'Dear lady, I am sorry that the conversation was not as amusing as one would have hoped. That man is a fiend. Quite unlike Theo's typical Sundays. We shall have to meet again, *sans* that scurrilous fellow. I know Theo was delighted to make your acquaintance.'

Since she had uttered hardly a word in that strange drawing room, Lily doubted this, but she murmured something pleasant, then Bartholomew returned to the house for a private chat with Theo, and she and Nicholas were finally off on their own again.

In the car, he observed, 'Theo's a bit of a fraud, you know. The house is a fake, his title is fake—'

'That blowsy painting *must* be a fake,' she said, laughing.

'Absolutely!'

They continued on in silence for a while. Then, 'They all know you,' she murmured, 'and they seem to like you.'

'It's the restaurant. Theo is a kind of gastronome, and my place, Heaven forbid, has become stylish. I wouldn't say I object to being something of a celebrity chef, since it brings in the money, but at times it's embarrassing.' He paused. 'Theo reads your column. He liked you back there, I could tell.'

'That nice woman in the red dress – she likes *you*.'

They smiled at each other. Nicholas said, 'Sylvie is married. To Theo's brother.'

'Oh.' After another brief silence, she ventured, 'I found Theo a bit leaden, or sullen or something. My mother was irascible, so choleric types don't appeal to me very much.'

Again they smiled. Still looking at the road, he suddenly clasped her right hand, as he had done on Theo's brocade couch, only this time he brought it to his lips. A tremor passed through her like some shuddering, silver filament. His profile was so stern, she wanted to touch the fine bones of his cheek and jaw, and after a shy moment she did so, releasing her hand from his and passing her fingers lightly over the side of his face.

They had come into Dublin. She said softly, 'Savage isn't a Jewish name.'

'No. I said that to protect you from his hideousness. I was thinking you could be Jewish, with your Russian ancestry.'

Lily hesitated; then, all of a sudden, in the ashen darkness of the car, the truth seemed to insist on itself. For so long she had put on every form of motley, while her true colours had lain in the deepest closet of her being. But now she said, 'I am a mixture. Yes, my Russian grandfather is Jewish, though he doesn't like to say so. His wife was also Russian, only an ordinary Orthodox Russian. She died long before I was born, but in photos she looks very Russian, with her face all smooth planes, the cheeks flowing straight up to the eyes, you know? My father's grandfather was Irish, Cork-born, and my father's grandmother came from Liguria.'

Nicholas exclaimed, 'You seem to embody nearly the whole story of early twentieth-century American immigration!'

She laughed. 'You could look at it that way.'

He went on, in the kind of yearning voice with which people speak of some happy memory from their vanished childhood. 'And the food! It must have been splendid: Italian, Russian, Jewish . . .'

'My mother— ' she began, then faltered. After a moment she said, 'When the Nazis decreed that Danish Jews must wear the Star of David, the King of Denmark and his courtiers came out to hunt the next morning all wearing Stars of David. You reminded me of the King of Denmark this evening, saying Savage is a Jewish name.' Once more she paused. 'I'm not really afraid, or ashamed, to reveal my Irish or Italian or Russian Orthodox sides. But I *am* reluctant to expose that I'm one-quarter Jewish.'

'Why?' he asked softly.

'I suppose because my grandfather was – is – a bit of an anti-Semite. He lived and breathed the ballet. It's a world of fantasy, of magic, and he was ravished by it. He wanted to be Russian the way Diaghilev and Nijinsky were. The Jewish part was – an inconvenience.'

'What about your mother?' Nicholas asked. How does *she* feel, about her Jewish side?'

Lily looked out of her window, at the lighted terrace of a pub where three young women, all with long blonde hair and bronzed complexions, were drinking flutes of champagne. 'She disliked my grandfather's pretensions, his vodka-and-caviar routine, the French phrases he liked to let drop, how he behaved as if his ancestors were White Russians from Saint Petersburg who travelled to their dacha in a sleigh when they weren't appearing at Court. So she embraced her American suburban world with a kind of vehemence. It was like she was the typical rebellious artist child in reverse. She rebelled by becoming conventional, though she can be as histrionic as my grandfather, in her own way . . . ' Another pause. 'Anyway, she's never concealed her Jewishness. In fact I think at times she has *displayed* it, in order to embarrass him. But I— ' She gave an abashed smile. 'I don't want to be like my mother. I always wanted to be like my grandfather. I've never understood how she can live without beauty.'

They had halted at a red light; he extended two fingers and touched the highest point of her cheekbone. 'She *has* lived with beauty.'

Lily felt herself blush. 'Thank you. But I mean her life, our life, was unlovely. Our house looked like every other house on the street. There was no grace in our circumstances. Do you know what I mean?'

Still in that low voice, he said, 'Yes. I know precisely what you mean.'

He stopped the car at the Arts Club door. The street was still. He gave her a light kiss, just brushing her lips.

Then, 'Listen,' he said, almost gruffly, 'Why don't you come to my flat, Wednesday night? It's my night off, and I would like to cook dinner for you. Will you come?'

'Yes,' she whispered. And she kissed *him* this time, only more firmly. His hand moved down her shoulder and glanced along her breast. Then she broke the embrace, and left the car, she did not know how – or why – beyond a feeling that *the time had not yet come*, and was hurrying up to the front door, calling good-bye to him.

Chapter III

Last night I dreamt of my parents' house, which had been my house, too, although how eager I had been to escape it, with its cargo of bitter memories!

Only, lately I return there, every night in dreams. And last night when I could not sleep I made a conscious effort to remember, to recall the outside of the house and every one of its rooms, and how it had felt to be myself within it.

First there was . . . let's see . . . there was a path through a small garden where a frail tree stood. Then one of those mesh doors so common in America, to keep the insects out in summer. I used to press my face against that metal web from the outside, looking in at my own living room altered, darkened, as though I were gazing at it through a thicket. (In the hot months the inner door, the real one, would be left open, and the mesh one fastened closed with a hook on the inside, for security I suppose, although I cannot recall much fear of crime in those more innocent years.) The fragile, hollow squeal, a kind of whingeing sound, that mesh doors make when they are opened or closed, still echoes in my dreams. It is not a happy sound, for me.

The living room. At noon in summer the distant keen of a siren, while a plank of sunlight, clouded with motes, falls in through the window. A television, books, a pleasant smell of furniture polish. Everything very still, except for the whirring of the grandfather clock as it prepares to strike the hour. I suffered from hay fever, so I sought refuge in that room from the world of harsh sunlight and pollen and children scrambling over grass, refuge in the sudden coolness and dimness, the green sofa on which I would sprawl to read my favourite books: *Gone With The Wind*, illustrated biographies of Mary, Queen of Scots and Joan of Arc. But it had other aspects.

Evening and the din of the television: why did my father automatically, invariably, turn the thing on, and leave it on, even after the six o'clock news? I hear it and hear it in my mind's ear, ceaseless, mindless, a kind of squalor of noise. My mother has made dinner. I have laid the table. My father and I eat (steak? roast chicken? lamb chops? she was not a bad cook) while my mother stays in the kitchen, drinking gin and 'giving out', as the Irish say.

Specific memories. Yes, one of those nights. My father and I pass plates, eat meat and drink water constrainedly, while the television squawks behind. My mother has come in from the kitchen and has settled on her chair at the round dining table, though not to eat. She is brooding, immobile, except for the hand that mechanically raises the glass or the cigarette. Her eyes stare straight ahead. Her coarsening face, the fug of gin and smoke surrounding her, the heavy silence that seems to fume from her, make her resemble a basilisk (I am not exaggerating). What do we do, my hapless father and myself, beside that rigid presence? Does the food curdle in our stomachs; do we make stilted conversation?

What age am I?

But let us return to the living room. My father and I have finished our meal. (Dessert is out of the question, as was a starter. One course was nearly, though not quite, endurable. If meals are sacraments then ours were a black mass.) My father is in his armchair, reading the newspaper, although the television continues to blast away. I have returned to my favourite sofa, to do homework, I suppose, or bury my apprehensive head in a book. This is when the onslaught begins, this is the moment when she is oiled with enough gin to launch into her particular kind of tirade. But why do I not leave? Why do I huddle on a chair, clutching a book on which I cannot focus? It is probably not yet dusk; I have friends, why do I not fly from that sordid house? Why do I not *go out and play*?

Now, appallingly, she eats. The food has grown cold, the fat and sauces have congealed, but she is not mindful of this. From the living room I stare with a mixture of repugnance and fascination while she feeds, still granite-faced, pushing cold meat, cold potatoes or cold spaghetti into her mouth, pausing only to swallow a mouthful of gin or to mutter. My dad tries to ignore her. Finally she puts down the cutlery and her voice rises again. She shouts, growls, roars. I do not go out. Her legs are sprawled wide, her face is red and swollen, her mouth a sewer. Why does my father not help me; why does he not cry, '*Enough!*'?

For I am the object of her rage. The air is foul with it. But I do not go out. I am told that I am a *fucking* this and a *goddamned* that (it is all a blur) and while she roars in this fashion, she takes a respite now and again to tilt back her head and blow out cigarette smoke with an affected and repellent delicacy. As if she were on stage.

Perhaps I do not go out because, helpless and befouled, I fear that I would surely take the dark things with me. Surely the blackness she was pouring into my heart had become my own, and how could I carry it out into the playgrounds, that darkness of the heart, like a black rose; how could I bear such a burden? Somewhere, in the ash-coloured twilight, children were collecting fireflies in glass jars, clambering up trees, dressing their dolls, pushing each other on swings. But I must stay in that room and hear the things she calls me, because only she, who laid the curse, has the power to lift it. She, who has soiled me, might, if I am lucky, also redeem me. And so I waited, hoping that she would relent, hoping for mercy. For grace. In other words, I believed her.

Ah, there it is. My answer, finally. That is why I did not go out. She was my mother, and I believed her.

Besides, there was, I must admit, the thrill of it. The moment would arrive when she'd finally fall silent, and wearily, blearily, go to bed. Or else continue. And at those times I would realise, with a shuddering in the region of my belly, a genuine *frisson*, that *she would stop at nothing*. Her transports of rage, her ecstasies of fury, her self-debasement, would know no bounds. Yes, I must admit that it fascinated me; how could it not? It was frightening yet strangely moving: Love and Dread in a head-on collision. What would she do next? What filth would she bellow? Would she strike me? Would I – I wondered with a shudder of delicious terror – strike back? Her drink-loosened legs open wider and wider as she droops in her chair: frowsty, stinking of gin. She is obscene, and I watch as she turns on my father and begins to revile *him*, throws a glass or a plate at him, tries to beat him with her fists when, finally, he has approached her in an attempt to calm her down, a kind of parody of the devoted husband wooing his wife with passionately extended arms . . .

It is curious that I should have become a restaurant critic, because as a child I feared my appetites. I was slight, with strange looks, a cloud of hair and wide solemn eyes, like some forest creature in a storybook. In old photographs, my face, encircled by that nimbus, seems always startled and small. My mother, on the other hand, was large, or seemed large, an exceedingly plump (though not quite fat) woman. She spoke loudly, seldom troubling to modulate her rather deep voice, and her appetites were voracious. She drank, ate and talked excessively; as for her sexual appetite, whatever was happening between my father and her was a mystery, and one I would not really like to unravel.

Yet now I wonder how her indelicacies might have affected the growth of my own sexuality. I was terrified of being like her and sometimes experienced myself as gross and clumsy, despite my smallness, as though she had somehow managed to invade my body and bloat me like a frog. Once, when I was quite young, maybe five or six, the teacher organised our class into a circle for dancing, the kind of merry, innocent dance taught in American schools then. But as I capered hand-in-hand with a small boy called Harold, I felt – how vividly I remember the sensation – I felt big, coarse, and my cheeks burned with consternation, even though I was certainly smaller than little Harold, indeed than most of the children in my class.

Ah, but yes, I do recall that feeling, as though it were yesterday, my body thickening, its movements growing stupid, as I stumbled round the schoolroom with Harold, who seemed so graceful, and whose light hand in mine shamed me, as if I were *her*, as if I had become *her*.

Of course the trouble really started when I reached puberty. Obviously, such a mother would not have made that particular passage easy. Anyway, at age fourteen or so, *I closed down*. That is the only way I can describe it. When my body changed, I fell under a kind of swoon or spell. Sex ceased to matter. It *had* mattered earlier: at age ten or eleven, long before I'd needed such advice, I had begun to read the silly magazines designed for older girls, full of prattle about make-up, boys and the woes of adolescence. But when I should have opened my eyes, I closed them, no longer smoking illicit cigarettes with friends in dark cellars, or accompanying boys there, to experiment with awkward kisses. Something had frightened me, had turned me chaste as an anchorite.

My grandfather, taking me out for sumptuous meals at the Russian Tea Room, did not detect my new remoteness. He was too busy visiting all his ambitions on me, his only granddaughter, whose temperament was like his own, who would curve back to Europe, and flourish for him there. He would stare at me with his fierce eyes, registering my eccentric looks, savouring the future he believed they would create for me, how I would surely do something bohemian and splendid – unlike my mother. He did not perceive that I was slumbering, that I had taken refuge in books and daydreams, perhaps because he also lived in a world of dreams.

So there we were, my imperious grandfather with his straight dancer's back, and myself, unformed and dreamy, seeing nothing peculiar in our dinners of caviar and blini, or the thimbles of vodka, perfumed with fruit, that he let me drink although I was so young. Yet we must have looked and sounded pretty bizarre, this old man and adolescent girl at a restaurant table, talking raptly about Diaghilev, Nijinsky, Benoit and Bakst, Cocteau and Monte Carlo. I suppose such romantic meals and conversation were as close to a sexual awakening as I could manage then.

But what about my grandfather? Was he not bored, after all? He was used to the company of *soignée* ballerinas, of choreographers and artists. Perhaps he did know we made an odd couple; perhaps he was simply giving me a respite from my mother, whose drunkenness he must have been aware of even though we never spoke of it – no one spoke of it. Just as we never spoke of how fey and solitary I had become.

How I emerged from my chrysalis is an obvious enough story. I went away, far from my mother and father, and discovered girls first, warm friendships that were faintly erotic. Those soul talks at my English school, where we sprawled all evening on rumpled beds, eating chocolates or smoking forbidden pot and unburdening our callow hearts, were not entirely innocent. And then there was the first boy, an ordinary schoolboy though very nice, who touched the place in me that was green and alive – I had not even known it was there – but afterwards I could not lose myself in sleep again.

As far as food was concerned, I believe that I always had what might be called a discerning palate, even as a child, long before I went to Nice with Vivian and her parents. During an interminable suburban afternoon, while my mother was still sleeping it off and my father was absorbed in an old film on the television, I would make myself a meal of good cheese, French bread and sweet butter, perhaps with a surreptitious half-glass of wine poured from an opened bottle standing on the counter. I would eat solemnly, alone, in the kitchen; it was one of my private ceremonies, of which I had many.

There is a memory, very strong, from when I was quite small, seven or eight, perhaps? Three or four older boys approach me where I am idling on the swings in a little concrete playground. It is a hot day. The air smells of tarmac; the metal ropes of the swing nearly scorch my palms. I twirl round to twist those ropes; then swing back in the other direction to unravel them. The boys bear gifts: bags of sweets ('candy', I should say); stalks of red liquorice; multi-coloured lozenges pierced in the middle and threaded on cords to make edible necklaces; a packet of the soap-flavoured candy called Violets which, for some mysterious reason, maybe *because* of the horrible flavour, we children love. Dangling candy necklaces before my nose, the boys look like a picture I saw recently at school, of the suave Dutch governor offering a casket of trinkets to the Indians of Manhattan. We schoolchildren were told those noble-looking natives would barter their island for twenty-four dollars worth of rubbish.

The boys, who are, perhaps, only nine or ten, inform me they will give me all their candy if I go with them to the cellar of a nearby apartment house, and take down my pants. They will only *look*, they assure me; they *won't touch*. They *promise*. This seems a fairly reasonable deal.

I remember, still, the descent, a smell of damp, the boys clustering eagerly at the top of the stairs, dim against the rectangle of sunlight behind them, one the official look-out, glancing right and left. In the narrow oubliette below, surrounded by stone and spiders, I oblige them, lowering my pants and displaying first the moon of my bottom, and then my little girl's groin.

Well, they honoured their promise, and presently off I went, back to the hot, empty playground, my hands full of ill-gotten candy. What I had done seemed not to trouble me as I went about my child's business, scuffling over the tarmac in my sandals then settling once more on the swings, where I spread the sweets over my bruised knees and contemplated them with pleasure. But some years later, in dreams, the hot brown hands of the boys *touched* my white thighs, and after such dreams I was left with a memory of wet stone, and a confusion of lust and shame. I decided that other little girls would not have agreed to such a bargain, would not have displayed themselves obscenely for a bit of candy, would not have been so brazen. I was, after all, without modesty. Despite my attempts to escape, I was my mother's daughter . . .

*

Lily brought wine, one bottle of Mâcon-Lugny and another of a dark Mont de Ventoux. Nicholas lived in Donnybrook, in a flat decorated with modern, presumably Irish paintings: a giant fish; a dreamy landscape. He kissed her at the door, again just touching her lips with his, and brought her into the kitchen. It was large and seriously well-appointed, as she had expected, with pots of herbs on the window, and baskets of onions, shallots, ginger, brown eggs and bluish duck eggs, avocados and artichokes, arranged along the counter. Ropes of garlic, and green and red chillies, hung from the ceiling, and below them a plate of cheeses – a herb-encrusted goat's cheese, a chunk of West Cork Coolea, some coulant brie, a piece of craggy parmesan – ripened on a small table beside the black-and-silver professional oven.

She settled at the kitchen table, laid with cutlery and large goblets; he poured her some white wine, a pale Meursault, and said, 'I'll work here for a while longer, cooking the starter. But do talk to me, if you don't mind speaking to my back.'

She liked *looking* at his back, his dark hair and slender nape, broad shoulders and sharp shoulder blades, those arms. *He is so strong*, she observed, as she had done in Roundwood, and suddenly felt slightly light-headed, as if from the wine, though she had barely touched it.

He had put on an apron over khaki trousers and a yellow shirt. As for her own clothes, she was wearing a rather eccentric black dress, high-waisted in the Empire style, cut low and square at the top, with long sleeves and a long skirt. Her hair, which had grown and now touched her shoulders, she had gathered up into a kind of haphazard chignon. She gazed at him without speaking while he sharpened a knife, moving it swiftly back and forth across the whetstone. Suddenly he smiled over his shoulder, and asked '*Ça va?*'

'*Ça va*,' she echoed softly. He took up the sharpened knife and began to unfurl the papery skin of a shallot, and then to cut it on a wooden board. Also on the board was a cluster of blanched asparagus, and a mass of chopped sweetbreads, all soft and furrowed. He dropped the shallot into a pan heating on the cooker at his elbow; it sizzled, and a smell of hot butter rose from it, seeming almost to burnish the air. Then he swept in the sweetbreads, the asparagus, and some green herb – tarragon, she thought – and the pan flared and hissed. After a moment he splashed in a little Madeira from a bottle beside him on the counter, and the pan sizzled yet again, releasing a rich caramel scent. Finally he lowered the flame almost to nothing, and came to sit beside her, pouring himself a glass of wine.

'It won't be long now,' he said, and then, not so unexpectedly, extended his hand and caressed the side of her face. Staring at him, she seized the hand where it lay on her cheek, and brought it to her lips. His fingers were fragrant with tarragon.

'Lily,' he said, 'I even dream about you.'

He stood up, returning to the cooker, and finished the sauce with a soupcon of cream so rich that it was nearly solid. Then he came back with the sweetbread and asparagus fricassee arranged prettily on two small blue plates. He poured them more wine, and settled at the place beside her again.

She ate seriously, with pleasure, despite her shyness and yearning for him; in fact, the flavours of the dish were a good distraction, stilling, at least for the moment, the schoolgirl tremor in her body.

Suddenly he jumped up, and brought over two more plates that had been waiting on a counter by the fridge. 'Look,' he said excitedly, almost babbling, 'I've made another starter. I always prepare two, a hot one and a cold. You'll like this; it's red mullet – the French say rouget – raw but marinated in lemon juice, like ceviche. The thick sauce underneath is a kind of rouille, full of seared red peppers, but softened with olive oil, and that timbale beside it is an aspic of bouillabaisse; really, I cooked a proper bouillabaisse and then jellied it.'

He was hectic – with nerves, she thought – but obviously with the enthusiasm of a real cook as well. 'Try this bit,' he cried, 'the acid in the lemon juice actually cooks the rouget, and the rouille has a bit of fennel in it. Do you like it?'

'It's lovely, lovely,' she answered between mouthfuls, and it *was* delicious, the cold salty bouillabaisse, the rouille lush with chillies and fennel, the utterly fresh red mullet. 'I have never eaten food like this, Nicholas. It is so rich and startling.' She laid down her cutlery. He was staring at her.

'The main course is a Spanish fish stew,' he said slowly. 'It's nearly all made. I must just heat it up, and put the mussels in, and a bit of parsley, and some sherry.'

'Let me help you.' She rose at the same moment as himself; they were both holding full glasses, and somehow they stumbled against each other and her hand was jostled, spilling wine over the bodice of her dress.

'Oh, no,' he exclaimed, seizing a tea towel, 'I'm sorry. Your pretty dress.'

'It doesn't matter. It's only white wine. It doesn't matter.'

But he was smoothing the towel over her naked throat and the top of her breasts, glistening with spilled wine above the black fabric. His hand did not touch her. She fell silent.

'You should take it off,' he said in a strange, rough voice, 'You should take it off, or you'll be cold.'

She smiled: Men! Asking you to *remove* your clothes, or you'll be cold. But, 'You do it,' she whispered, 'You take it off.'

His fingers, fumbling with the buttons, finally touched her breasts; his face was soft with concentration, a wing of dark hair curving across his cheek. The dress dropped to the floor. She reached behind, unfastened her bra, and let it fall as well.

She registered with interest that her knees were actually buckling, like the heroine of some mawkish romance novel, so that when he rescued her from falling along with her clothes, by taking her in his arms, she was relieved as well as excited. She wrapped her arms round his shoulders and he kissed her hard on the mouth. His hands were moving slowly over her body, pushing down her pants as she eased off her shoes, until she was completely naked while he remained fully clothed, even to the apron.

She began, urgently, to undress him, and after she had tugged off the apron and unbuttoned his shirt, he swung her up in his arms with no effort at all, and carried her out of the kitchen and into the bedroom, where he put her down on the bed, covered with a black duvet.

'You are so *white*,' he said in that same strange thick voice, 'like Devonshire cream.'

'Not *everything* has to do with food,' she admonished playfully, reaching up for him, but a few minutes later, contradicting her own reproach, she gasped, 'What about the Spanish fish stew?'

'We can have it later,' he whispered into her ear, 'It only gets better with time.'

They did actually eat the Spanish fish stew. It must have been about midnight, or even one or two; there was a deep, slumbering feeling to the darkness beyond his window. But she had lost all sense of time. There was only the lighted kitchen, and the smells of garlic and saffron and brine, this last smell coming from the mussels and fish in the stew and also from her own salted skin. And there was only himself, a blue dressing gown thrown carelessly over his body (he had given her a sort of boxer's robe to wear, made of white towelling, but she had not fastened it closed) and the bottle of wine between them on the table, the bowls of peppery stew, the homemade bread. He said, 'Tell me more about yourself. Are your parents still alive, and your extraordinary grandfather?'

She had been so drowsily happy, but now the familiar tension returned. She was composing one of her cautious replies when he went on, 'Did your mother cook Russian food? There's a Georgian recipe, cabbage stuffed with meat and cinnamon, that I'd like to try.'

She laughed. If all he wanted was information about Russian cuisine, she could oblige him honestly enough. Yes, she said, certain Russian flavours were familiar to her: the mouth-puckering pickled vegetables, herrings marinated in sour cream and icicles of raw onion, cabbage soup, pumpernickel bread.

But she wanted to vouchsafe him more than descriptions of Baltic food. So she continued to tell him about her grandfather, how he was still alive but frail now, much diminished, no longer an autocrat with fiery eyes but a little brown wren of a man, at least in photographs, since she had not seen him for many years. And about how she had worshipped him as a child because the world of ballet dancers was like some hothouse full of luxuriant flowers. She was silent a moment. And then she surprised herself by saying, 'My mother was – she had a problem with drink. And I think he might have been responsible for her drinking, at least to some degree, because he was so terribly narcissistic. In his youth he was beautiful in the way some dancers are, and probably insufferable! I think he might have been a rather heartless father . . . '

She stopped, taken aback by her own revelations. She had not known she was feeling these things, but, once uttered, they were *there*, unassailably. And picturing her mother as a child, at the mercy of such a temperamental man, Lily suddenly remembered a scene from her own past, of her grandfather trying to teach her to dance. She must have been very young, perhaps only six, but she had tried to please this haughty master, twirling and bowing at his command. 'Leap!' he had cried, 'Pretend that the carpet is a babbling brook and *leap* gracefully over it!' But it hadn't worked, she had continued to thump rather than to leap, and he had scowled in bitter disappointment. She recalled now how she had waited, breathing heavily, while he turned away, even his back rigid with scorn. How *stupid* she had felt in her tights and slippers, ashamed, as when she had danced with Harold in the schoolroom. Of course he had warmed to her again – after it had become clear she would grow up to be handsome – but that other harsh grandfather must have been the one with whom her mother had lived.

And no doubt there had also been the dark side of his bohemian world. It had been fine for Lily, who saw her grandfather now and again, for good meals and theatrical conversation. But her mother would have been at the beck and call of Jacob and his whimsical friends, the vain ballerinas who would have ignored a little girl, the megalomaniac choreographers and conductors. There would have been strange visitors at strange hours, meals thrown together at three in the morning, with Lily's mother lying stiffly in bed, desperate for sleep after she had prepared her books and folded her clothes on a chair in preparation for school the next day. Jacob's wife had died when their daughter was a baby: who had prepared the child's breakfast, tied her shoelaces? How many mornings had she cried for an egg or a bit of toast, while Jacob gossiped with a petulant ballerina who had dropped in without notice, or slept on and on after a night's carousing, the sky growing forlornly bright, the child waiting at the kitchen table, afraid to rouse him? This was the life Lily's mother had known. Only Lily hadn't fully realised this, had not actually felt sad for her mother, until just now.

She realised something else, as well. There were things she was still not prepared to reveal to Nicholas, things that had nothing to do with the world of ballerinas, but with the dark cellars of the mind and heart. And this, she realised, was partly the reason for her lifetime of deceit. She was afraid that if anyone – if Nicholas – glimpsed how black with rage her heart was, he would be horrified, might even be destroyed. Yes, monsters were born of such death-dealing fury as she harboured in her heart, and therefore she had mastered evasion, so that those she loved, looking into her black eyes, would not die of shock. And yet many children must fear, as she had feared, that one glimpse of her anger could kill her parents, while, at the same time, that other voice was whispering, *I want them to die, to die . . .*

'Does your mother still drink?' asked Nicholas softly.

'No. She gave it up soon after I left for school in England; she had to. It was ruining her health. But by that time the harm had been done. To me, I mean, though the damage to her health also remains.'

'Are there any good things, pleasant things, you remember about your parents?'

Lily smiled. Paradoxes! A bohemian grandfather who was also a kind of dictator, a mother who hungered for respectability while flying into drunken rages. How many times had she shuddered at the memory of that frowsty woman and her placatory husband, their dull house? Yet her mother and father had also tutored her in a kind of sweetness, 'believe it or not', had been playful, and had had some of the courage of those who emerge from the working and immigrant classes, a quality she could only describe as rue. She tried to convey this to Nicholas, and then said, 'Now it's your turn, please. What was it like to grow up in Belfast?'

He pushed their bowls to the side, brought over the plate of cheeses, and poured out more wine.

'It's strange you should talk about class, because where I grew up it was on everybody's mind, all the time, class and religion. We lived close to the sea, in a working-class part of Belfast – all wee houses, dour streets, and those terrible murals. It was Protestant, very Protestant. And full of a kind of desperate attempt at gentility. My mother was appalled by the Catholics with their holy pictures in the house, but she stuffed our house with the same kind of kitsch, only it was Coronation jugs and Royal Family tea towels instead of Sacred Hearts. Over everything, over all my childhood, were those enormous Harland and Wolff gantries. And always the talk of my four uncles, who were in the shipping business. They would come for tea, and I would stand at the corner of the oilcloth, listening to their stories. Once Uncle Billy told my mother, "I swear to you, we never pushed the Catholics into the furnace, like they did in the Bible. We only threw them into the sea now and again, to freshen them up." And he laughed and laughed.'

Nicholas ate a piece of cheese. She did not speak. She was conscious of their bodies within the loose dressing gowns, still warm from lovemaking, and her hands wanted to touch him again. It didn't matter that she was satisfied from their hours in bed; he was rekindling her again with his serious face, his lovely chest and

Elizabeth Wassell

hands, and his story of an early life in some ways like her own: a lonely child, a barren house, a dearth of grace.

He went on, 'I was clever, so I got a scholarship and was sent to a rather posh Protestant secondary school. Only, of course, they never forgot where I came from, and presumed I'd be a rugby star. I didn't mind *looking* at rugby, but I loathed playing it, so I was pretty miserable at school until I made friends with a boy in my year, a Chinese boy called Jonah Chen. You mustn't forget Belfast in the nineteen-seventies was like every other town in the UK, with ethnic minorities pouring in, so that alongside the Taigs and Prods there was this new population of Indians and Chinese: the Empire circling back to Britain. The Chinese were mainly Methodists whose ancestors had been converted by missionaries – my school was Methodist so there were a fair number of Chinese. And they knew how to cook!'

'Was your own mother a good cook?'

'God, no. Her cooking was part of the whole depressing place, like those dank streets, and the picture of the Queen, and the cuckoo clock on the mantel. All the rooms smelled of boiled cabbage and old fat. She never cleaned the fry pan, and she re-used the cooking oil until it was nearly black. So her Ulster fries were encrusted with something like soot, and she would do the eggs hard as bullets. We had bread and marge every day for tea. The big meal was at one o'clock, and it was always a fry – I still can't bear those starchy Irish sausages – or overcooked chops. And there was always the bottle of brown sauce, and tea strong as iron.'

He laughed grimly. 'Then, one day, Jonah brought me home for dinner, a big family dinner made by his uncle who had been a famous chef in China. The uncle let Jonah and me into the kitchen to watch him cook. I had never seen or smelled such things: Chinese broccoli, ginger, coriander, little glistening dumplings full of pork or seafood, ducks marinated in soya sauce, a whole fish cooked with scallions and black beans. And the way he chopped and scalloped the vegetables, and fried them in sesame oil with a handful of cashews, and prepared the meats and fish with spices I had never heard of. It was, literally, another world; it was a million miles away from khaki-coloured peas and brown sauce and my dad coming in all red-faced from the pub to stuff himself with potatoes.'

She said quietly, 'It was like that for me, too. There was the lonely world of home with its sordid meals, my mother screaming. And then I discovered this other world of foreign cities with their cafés and restaurants, their delicious food and wine, and people who ate and drank, and laughed and talked, with courtesy and style. A beautiful world where meals were a ritual bordering on the religious. That's why I loved restaurants, why I still love them.'

He touched her cheek, whispering something, some endearment; she couldn't hear. Then he said, 'Soon after that meal at Jonah's house, one of my uncles was at our kitchen table, and he asked me would I want to work on a ship when I grew up, like himself. And I said that I wanted to be the cook on a ship, that I would cook splendid Chinese food for all the sailors. My uncle's face went white. He was sure he had a nancy boy in the family.'

She did not answer. She was overcome with a strong feeling in addition to desire; it seemed to press on her heart, her throat, and she thought that it might be love. He reached towards her again and pushed the dressing gown back over her shoulders. Moving to his chair, she settled on his knee, wound her arms about his shoulders and kissed him. 'Are there any good things you remember about *your* family?'

He was smoothing his hand over her breasts and stomach. 'Yes. A kind of – of rough tenderness. The way my mother would kiss me, brusquely, you know, but with this shyness about it. My people were proud of being no-nonsense. You weren't supposed to talk about feelings. So when they expressed affection it was sort of blundering and childlike, and endearing in a way. When my father was pleased with me or my younger brother, he would just stand there, clutching his hat. Low-church Ulster fathers didn't kiss their children then. But I could see the pleasure in his face.'

'Oh, Nicholas,' she murmured. She didn't know what else to say. And as though he too were overcome, he also spoke no more, only lifted her in his arms as he had done earlier, and carried her to bed again. And again there were no words for a while.

As dawn was breaking, she got up to go to the loo. Nicholas was sleeping deeply. In the bathroom she caught a glimpse of her own image in the full-length mirror, and remembered how, as a child, she had considered herself shambling and clumsy, despite her elfin slightness. Now she turned back to the glass and examined her reflection. She had grown up to be tall, with a rounded figure. Her roundness (Hugo had likened her to a Degas) used to dismay her, but these days she was comfortable enough with her body. Certainly its capacity to give and receive pleasure had delighted her tonight. Almost bashfully, she touched the mirror with her fingers, as though to bless or console the woman reflected there, with her rumpled curls, and her becalmed eyes.

Chapter IV

Aquavit
Temple Bar
by Lily Murphy

Regional palates vary as much as any other aspect of culture. For instance, the Japanese palate is inclined towards fish, pungent broths and pickled vegetables. The northern French palate responds to butter, cream, soft cheeses, gentle herbs, the Greek to salty cheeses, olive oil, oregano and garlic.

The Scandinavian palate is a piquant one, undaunted by sour condiments like mustard and vinegar. In fact there is a sauce for marinated salmon made simply with mustard, oil, vinegar, a bit of sugar and lots of fresh dill. It has the velvety texture of a mayonnaise despite the absence of eggs, only its flavour is much more tangy, lovely with oily fish like salmon or herrings.

Aquavit, the newest restaurant in Temple Bar, abounds with such peppery, biting flavours. There is a vast hors-d'oeuvres table (or, of course, smörgåsbord) arrayed with smoked and marinated salmon; herrings in sour cream and dill; seafood terrines; a dish called kottfarssvepta agg, which is a kind of Scotch egg; as well as vegetable dishes like pickled mushrooms and cucumber salad.

This splendour was a far cry from my most recent Nordic culinary experience. Last week, a friend and I visited a man who adores the Arctic. (Sometimes I really believe Europe is divided between those who dream of the South, of vineyards and silver olive trees, and those haunted by the chilly and mysterious North.) Anyway, this man belongs to the latter group. He has lived for periods in Iceland and Greenland, mastering Faroese dialects, and once worked on a Norwegian herring boat. When we arrived at his house in Dalkey, he insisted we try a rare delicacy from Greenland; it was a ceremony of passage, he said, a kind of ritual welcome, to be toasted with glasses of aquavit.

'What *is* this ancient dish?' I asked.

'Ancient is correct,' he answered serenely. 'Whale. Very *old* whale.'

His wife cried, 'You are not eating decomposing whale in my kitchen. I don't care if it's raining. Take that rotten fish *outside my house.*'

So we put on yellow mackintoshes, our host seized the bottle of aquavit and three glasses – as well as a brown paper parcel which he anchored under his arm – and we proceeded out the back door.

It was a mizzling rain, the kind that cowls you in vapour and pearls on your eyelashes. It was a bit cold as well, but we were in good humour, huddled outside the scullery door in our yellow macs, drinking fiery aquavit from reddening hands, until our friend unfurled his now-damp package.

I cannot describe the smell. It was more acrid than mouldering meat, ranker than rancid fat.

'This is the supreme Faroese delicacy,' smiled our host. 'It's really, really high. This whale was buried for ages, marinating in its own juices. Those black thousand-year-old eggs they serve in China are *nothing* compared to this. Here, try a chunk.'

I took a piece in my fingers, examined its evil shimmer, breathed its rancid smell – and faltered. I could not bear to put it into my mouth, even a mouth anaesthetised by aquavit. 'It's impossible,' I sighed. 'I cannot perform this ceremony of passage. I have failed to honour your hospitality.'

The friend who had brought me blanched at his morsel as well, but luckily our host was not offended. 'Never mind,' he assured us, chomping on nuggets of putrid whale. 'Most people can't manage it. Let's go in before we get drenched. The wife made lamb. *Fresh* lamb. And don't let me forget to tell you about the new translation of Shakespeare's sonnets into Faroese.'

But back to Aquavit in Temple Bar. After that lavish smörgåsbord, the main courses are nearly a comedown.

(Actually, a great many restaurants of almost every nationality do better starters than mains. From antipasti to salade niçoise to Greek mezze, the small savoury dishes that precede a meal are often the best thing about it.) However, the main courses at Aquavit are interesting enough. There is a dish of boiled beef called pepparrotskott, garnished with horseradish. And you can choose from a variety of quite sophisticated meatballs, with sour cream, or in a sauce made tart with gherkins. The fish is quite good, as one would expect. Desserts include a plate of Scandinavian cheeses. The one called Jarlsberg, a hard nutty cheese similar to Gruyère, is particularly flavoursome. And there is a marvellous dish of cloudberries under billows of cream.

Of course there are Scandinavian beers, but also some excellent white wines to accompany the seafood that dominates the menu. I love white Burgundies because they are not shallow and sharp like many dry whites, but rich and deep as grain; the Chassagne-Montrachet offered here is lovely. And of course there is a fine selection of aquavits, unaccompanied, thank goodness, by foetid whale meat.

★

After their first night together, she would have stayed all day with him, but they both had to work. And since they would be out very late, he cooking, she reviewing a Thai restaurant in Kildare (in Athy, as a matter of fact), they decided to meet again the following evening. A sensible arrangement, but when she kissed him good-bye, a kind of wistfulness contracted her heart;

the day without him would pass slowly.

She resolved not to think about him until they met again, but almost as soon as she arrived back at the Arts Club her editor rang, to assign her a review of the Restaurant Matisse. She was to go there on a Monday night, in two weeks' time.

Laughing, she phoned Nicholas, who also laughed. 'It looks like the world is conspiring to keep us meeting. I'm glad it will be a Monday, since they're usually pretty calm. I'll get the last main course out by eleven, and then we can drink some wine and go home.'

'You mustn't let on that you know me, or prepare anything unusual for me, or at least not until *after* the meal. My professional integrity must not be tarnished, you see. I ought to have a dining companion, to try more dishes. Shall I invite Sylvie?'

'Do. She's very nice, beneath those mannerisms. And I hope to prepare something *very unusual* for you after the meal.' He seemed to hesitate, then, 'I miss you already,' he mumbled, in a gruff voice that reminded her of his father, how Nicholas had described him, awkward, clutching his hat, but blushing with pleasure.

*

Lily had greatly enjoyed at least certain aspects of her London life. Even after Hugo left, her loneliness was leavened by her work, that brash world of journalism, her typically world-weary and tough-talking colleagues, their perpetual air of urgency, along with a growing sense that she was building a reputation for herself. People were reading her column and even discussing it.

And the city unfurled on all sides. Her sense of its age, its great cargo of history, never dimmed: the street names that evoked medieval times (mummers and monks and ladies with pomanders); an unexpected greensward in the centre of town; ancient pubs and houses; the splendid river. These things delighted that part of her which had never loved the New World. The curve of an old stone street, with a church spire in the distance, would always thrill her so much more than any glimpse of prairie. She was in love with London, with England, with Europe. And she was an outsider, which perhaps pleased her most of all.

Though an unsummoned image would sometimes plunge her into confusion. Her love of London's parks had its origin in the 'magic park', where her father had taken her when she was small. For now and again they'd gone on walks together, just the two of them, shuffling through autumn leaves or clumping through snow, her face tilting up to look at him in his coat and muffler. He had been romantic to her then.

One evening they had walked some distance to a neighbouring town. It was really a village, though Americans seldom speak of villages. But this place was older, sweeter, than most of the suburban settlements thereabouts, with leafy roads, a few drowsy-looking houses and a pretty church. Lily could not recall having been there before. They halted at a shop where a bowed woman, her face furrowed as an old tree, served them ice creams. Then, further along, they discovered a wooded path that stopped abruptly at a clearing through which a little stream coursed.

It was nothing really, just a small field and a flow of water. But for Lily it was like a place from an older country, or an enchanted meadow in a storybook. And her father said it would be their 'magic park'. She half believed it had materialised for them alone, and that it would disappear when they left, along with the bowed woman and her shop.

So certain early memories were written on her heart, were the landscape of her dreams, spoke to her in her mother tongue. This was the part of herself, of everyone, that we do not choose. Still, she did believe one could also choose a life, that to some degree we *are* what we love and long for. And it was through love that she had chosen Europe.

And she had also chosen Hugo, though in a curious way she was relieved when he dropped her. Now she need no longer endure jealousy, confusion, doubt, all that *mess*. She could go to the pub with her colleagues after work, take long walks in the evening, visit galleries and the cinema. She could move composedly, like a happy ghost, through this city that she loved, much as she had floated through her adolescence.

A successful, bright young woman, she was living like someone older, excusing herself early from the pub or a party with colleagues, to wait at the bus stop in the soft London dusk alongside tired mothers and their children and old-age pensioners. When on assignment, she often dined alone, even though it would have been more practical to invite someone along. And certainly there were plenty of people who would have jumped at the chance to eat a free meal and drink a bottle of free wine with a woman they liked for something fetching and eccentric in her manner and her looks. But Lily did not encourage them.

There was a restaurant on the corner of her street that did an all-day breakfast, to which she found herself going by herself most Sundays, to eat eggs florentine and read the papers. Sometimes a man would interrupt her, chat to her and then suggest a concert or a film. But she nearly always said no.

Yet now she had embraced Nicholas almost immediately with something at once wanton and shy inside herself. She did not know why this was so. She did not know why it should be this man whom she trusted, but it was, it was. Looking at him, listening to his stories, making love with him, she trusted him. Or nearly. Very nearly. She did not yet trust him enough to stop fearing that she would one day expose the drunk and quarrelsome part of herself, and he would flee from her.

They took a taxi to the restaurant. Sylvie was wearing another vivid frock, bright blue this time, with a blue scarf and blue sandals. Lily had put on a white dress made of some gossamer fabric that seemed to float when she moved. She had found it in a second-hand clothing shop that was so small and so overflowing with velvets, laces, opera cloaks, evening gloves and satin gowns, it had reminded her of her grandfather's apartment the moment she walked in.

'It's in a little street behind the Westbury,' she told Sylvie as they alighted from the taxi, 'Very modest from the outside. You'd never know it was there.'

And then it occurred to her she could describe Nicholas's restaurant the same way. The house was narrow, Georgian, like every other house on this south Dublin street, yet once they entered, and walked along a short corridor to the dining room, it was as though they had been spirited to the warm south. She had half-expected Matisse reproductions, but what the designer had done instead was to celebrate the palette of Matisse, his jonquil-yellow, lapis and violet-black, gold and pale blue, all glowing on the walls and tablecloths. Immediately she thought of Nice: the sea; that cleansing sunlight; the golden houses; and the flavours of olives, garlic and sharp herbs.

The room was not very large, with a small kitchen concealed behind a panel. She pictured Nicholas in there, his hands chopping an onion or breaking an egg into a bowl. And she recalled her private knowledge of those hands that could do such public things as chop vegetables or season a sauce. These thoughts made her warm with pleasure. But she was aware also of an apprehension: there *was* the Nicholas whom she did not yet know, the 'celebrity chef', admired, no doubt, by many ladies, the Nicholas whose lips spoke courtesies to moguls and ministers, whose hand clasped the hands of artists and socialites. She suddenly felt clumsy next to the feline Sylvie as they were brought to their table and given menus.

'Leave it to Nicky,' declared Sylvie with a satisfied grin, 'These dishes look absolutely *gorgeous*. Whatever shall we have?'

'You can't have what *you'd* like to have,' Lily answered severely, 'you are obliged to have what *I* decree you must have, or I won't be able to write a proper review.'

'Too bad. Let's get lots of lovely wine, anyway.'

Lily focused on the menu. The starters were as intriguing as she had expected: escabeche of mackerel; carpaccio of wood pigeon; salad of duck confit and Japanese mushrooms; lobster terrine. And the main courses were just as daring: roast lamb with salsa romano; goose and foie gras risotto; grilled hake in a coriander and lime sauce; jumbo scallops with Persian vegetables.

Unable to decide, for the moment, which dishes to take, they ordered two kirs royale and observed their fellow diners. It being

Monday, only three other tables were occupied. Sylvie recognised one couple: a middle-aged red-haired television presenter with her husband, a journalist who wrote piquant columns for several newspapers.

'I don't know any of the others,' she admitted, her sharp eyes scouring the room, 'but don't they look frightfully yuppie-ish?' She threw up her hands. 'Oh, what is happening? I used think if you could characterise Dublin as a person, it would be a cheeky street urchin with a grubby face and a delicious grin. But now I'm afraid it's turning into a businessman with a mobile phone pressed up against his ear.'

Lily was liking Sylvie more and more. She could seem affected and even frivolous, but as the dinner progressed, her conversation deepened like the flavour of the wine in their glasses, and Lily grew increasingly impressed with her astringent sense of humour and her intelligence. She was from 'a decaying mansion' in a midland county, remote from beaches, but close to a large lake. (Lily recalled Bartholomew describing his family home as *mouldering*, and she pictured a secret Ireland with once-stately houses crumbling away, while ancient family retainers trudged through the rooms until they were found, dry as husks, in some corner.)

Sylvie continued, 'When I was small, I missed the romantic west, and also those rather lovely strands along the Irish Sea. It seemed moribund, my home, surrounded by fields for ages, and full of dreadful horsy types.' She laughed. 'But as I grew older I began to like my county, so still and separate, and so *ancient*. All the tourists swarm to the coastal places, but I was living in the deep middle of Ireland, the *omphalos*, if you see what I mean.'

'Where do you live now?' asked Lily, who was listening intently while at the same time writing in her little book, *Pâté deeply lobster-flavoured, and accompanied by asparagus decorated with a poached quail's egg and the kind of hollandaise made frothy with cream, called mousseline . . .*

Sylvie answered, 'In a delightful mews. Ballsy is good with houses, and he found this absolutely splendid little place for us. Do try a nibble of my wood pigeon. Doesn't Nicky have a fantastic flair?'

Lily could tell that she wanted to discuss Nicholas, and so she obliged by describing their visit to his friend, the man who'd served them the rotten whale meat. But she didn't want Sylvie to gossip about him: she had decided Nicholas himself should be the source of any information concerning his past. After all, she knew she was fragile, and she dreaded being wounded by some idle comment made by Sylvie. To divert her, she said, 'Try some of this asparagus. Do you think the sauce is too rich?'

While they were at their dessert, Nicholas appeared in the dining room, still wearing his chef's whites, and looking so handsome, her throat closed for a moment, with pleasure, but also, once more, a kind of shy fear. And when he made a sign to her, indicating by a tilt of his head that he must speak to some of the other diners first, before approaching their table, she sighed apprehensively. Other diners were often other women, hungry, perhaps, for more than his wood pigeon. Oh, would the ghost of her mother always haunt her in this way, assuring her with an acrid look, a drunken insult, that she did not deserve her heart's desire? And Nicholas *was* her heart's desire; she had to admit it. The age-old symptoms were there: the joy she felt in his company, the whole world shining like the marvellous light that glistens in the sky after rain; and how she missed him when they parted even for a day, the whole world darkening. Yes, she was caught; she loved him. But the red-haired television presenter was smiling eagerly up at him with scarlet-painted lips, the same lips between which his dishes had passed only moments before. *Perhaps she's stupid and vain*, Lily thought hopefully, before lowering her eyes to concentrate on her blue cheesecake which was not sweet, so that it was a bit like dessert and cheese at the same time.

Finally, Nicholas seized a chair from an empty table and came to theirs. Lowering himself beside Lily, he kissed her, and she brushed his wrist with her fingers. He signalled to a waiter, who brought over a bottle of Bandol and three fresh glasses. Looking about, Lily was surprised to see that all the other guests had left.

Nicholas lifted her arm from the table and displayed it to Sylvie. 'Doesn't Lily have the slenderest hand? I would moisten it with a lightly beaten egg, roll it in bread crumbs, and grill it gently. Delicious with white wine.'

'Not enough meat,' said Lily, regarding her thin fingers.

Sylvie said, 'That wouldn't matter. One would munch on the bones, like eating a quail.' Suddenly she stood, and threw her azure scarf over one shoulder. 'I must go, darlings, or my poor husband will *waste away* while I have been growing *fat* on your *marvellous* food, Nicky. No, please don't rise; you must have been on your feet for ages. *Je t'embrasse.*' She kissed him and then Lily, before sweeping out in her lissom way, with cries of gratitude to them both, and an invitation to her mews house for dinner the following week.

'Very subtle, our Sylvie,' Nicholas observed, 'I thank her for letting us be alone at last.' He kissed Lily's palm and then frowned at it. 'I don't really think I should cook your hand. Then I wouldn't have it to kiss, afterwards.'

She looked round at the empty room, the radiant colours darker now that the table candles had been blown out. 'Where are the staff?'

'I've sent them home. Would you like to see the kitchen?'

It was small and compact, with a great many hanging pots and pans, just as she had pictured it. 'A little cooking orchard,' she said.

He brought her over to a cluster of peppers – the conventional bulbous ones (yellow, red and green); but also tapering jalapeños; furrowed chipotles; char-coloured pasilla; long-stalked peperoncini; dagger-like piquin; along with some smallish puckered ones she had never seen before – that were lying on the counter. 'Did you know,' he said softly, 'that a man called Scoville devised a way of measuring the heat of peppers, called Scoville units. For instance,' he touched a fresh pepper, 'these sweet ones have zero Scoville units. But those jalapeños over there measure up to about five thousand.' Next he indicated the small wrinkled ones whose name she did not know. 'These are called habaneros, or Scotch bonnets, and they're so fiery, they can contain up to three hundred thousand Scoville units.' He put one in his palm before passing it over to her. They both gazed down at it. 'Enough to scorch your insides.'

'You've done that already, Nicholas.'

His grey-blue eyes regarded her; then, abruptly, he grasped her by the waist and lifted her up onto the counter, disturbing the peppers so they tumbled to the floor. At the same time her elbow struck a saucepan on the other side, so that it, too, toppled, with a terrific clatter. They began to kiss, and meantime another pot or pan somehow fell from the counter, with yet another crash, and they found themselves laughing at how the kitchen had come suddenly to life with a great metallic din.

Presently she laid her head on his shoulder; she was still on the counter, her legs wrapped round his waist, his arms encircling her. His nape smelled of basil, and, kissing it lightly, she marvelled at how vulnerable that part of the body was. 'Your food,' she said, 'Your food was delicious.'

'It *was* especially good tonight,' he said in a satisfied voice, 'because it was cooked with love. That makes a difference.'

'I know. My mother cooked with anger, we ate anger with our meat. Much nicer to eat love.'

He helped her down, and they began to gather up the fallen things. Nicholas rinsed the peppers and put them into the fridge. She regarded his serious face, thinking that he had more or less told her he loved her. And then she noticed how tired he looked.

Suddenly she pictured Les Halles as it must have been before the markets of Paris moved out to Rungis. The fishermen and butchers drinking onion soup below the spires of St Eustache while all about them the city slept. The bang of cageots as piles of trout, salmon, oysters, mussels, scallops, crayfish and crabs were laid out on the cobbles beside beef, charolais, the yellow-skinned chickens of Bresse, the rabbits, the pigs' trotters and heads, the sweetbreads and tripe.

And moving through that city within a city, under the changing sky, were the chefs, squeezing fruit or examining a cheese, bargaining loudly with the butcher, stopping for a coffee and a gulp of calvados in one of the market cafés. They would barely have slept after closing up their restaurants the night before, and then, as morning broke, they would return from the market to open their kitchens again, to design that day's menu, to prep for lunch, oversee the staff. And Nicholas's life was a version of the same thing. He would come back from cooking all day to make a midnight supper for her. He would drag himself up out of bed before dawn while she slept on. It was arduous enough to make room for *her* in his working day, let alone some phantom rival. Yet she still clung to adolescent fears.

Just then he turned to look at her. She swallowed. 'Me too,' she said. 'I mean, me too, concerning love.'

He came closer and touched her cheek again. 'You're a funny thing,' he said gently, 'You're a funny, shy, lovely thing.'

Chapter V

Hungry Grass
Dublin 4
by Lily Murphy

Let me explain, for those who may not know, that 'hungry grass' refers to the desperation of Famine victims who tore at the grass with their teeth, they were so ravenous, and who died with green-smeared mouths.

Concerning the Great Famine, dissenting voices clamour these days – revisionists, traditionalists, anti-British, British apologists – all interpreting and re-interpreting what 'really' happened. Because I am only partly Irish, that particular sorrow makes up just a portion of my ancestral freight. But I have travelled through Ireland, and seen *killeens* where children are buried. And I have journeyed through eerily silent regions, remote valleys where no Irish is spoken, as though the local voices, stricken and stilled during the Famine, remain so today. It seems to me that the suffering of that time is seared into the Irish consciousness despite the country's new prosperity.

Therefore it is hard to convey just how offensive Hungry Grass is as the name of a restaurant. Is this supposed to be a joke? Are we supposed to laugh, while we guzzle our wine and gobble our sirloin, at the memory of those who died eating grass? Perhaps we are meant to reflect, to feel abashed at our gluttony, our obscenely immense portions of gratin dauphinois, a far cry from the blighted spuds of yesteryear. If so, my fellow diners were certainly missing the point. Mostly couples (I'm afraid the place *is* romantic-looking, with candlelight and soft-footed waiters), they were eating up happily, clearly oblivious to any irony. At least there were no dishes called Potato Blight Soufflé or Soup Kitchen Potage.

Actually, the food here isn't bad, but it isn't great, either; it's just okay. Without the name, this would be a moderately okay city centre restaurant. But with the name, it's an unbelievably vulgar place with mediocre food. And expensive, as well.

By the way, 'hungry grass' also describes how you are said to feel when you walk over ground where a perishing famine victim once sprawled to eat the grass. You are supposed to be seized by hunger and weakness, by the anguish of the very man, woman or child who had lain where you are walking, their belly empty save for grass. When I walked into

Elizabeth Wassell

Hungry Grass, I experienced a seizure, all right, though not of hunger and weakness but only disgust.

I know I ought to fulfil my restaurant critic's duty by describing the dishes and wine and the prices, but I simply cannot bring myself to do so. Instead, I include an extract from a poem called 'The Hungry Grass', by Donagh MacDonagh:

> *Little the earth reclaimed from that poor body,*
> *And yet, remembering him, the place has grown*
> *Bewitched, and the thin grass he nourishes*
> *Racks with his famine, sucks marrow from the bone.*

★

Dear Madam,

I write to complain about Lily Murphy's most recent restaurant column in your magazine, more of a tirade really, against the Hungry Grass restaurant in Dublin 4. While I have always enjoyed Ms Murphy's reviews, I was appalled by her diatribe in last week's issue. Where has her sense of humour gone? As she herself comments, she is not really Irish (despite her name), so perhaps she does not understand that, at this point in our history, we would like to move beyond gloom, those images of keening old women and ruined cottages so dear to our grandparents. In other words, we are ready for a bit of fun, ready to laugh even at the sad bits of our history. I am not offended by a restaurant called Hungry Grass. But I am offended by Lily Murphy's dismissal of it, and her refusal to discuss the food and wine. One of the reasons I read her reviews is that I enjoy her descriptions of the dishes, and her often quite funny observations about the people surrounding her in the restaurant. And like most ordinary punters I want to know about the prices! But she has let her readers down this time, and I hope she won't force her extreme opinions down our throats (so to speak) in the future. After all, a woman who devotes her working life to the pleasures of the table should not accuse others of gluttony or insensitivity because they enjoy a meal in a restaurant. And I don't believe she has actually ever seen children's burial grounds or 'silent' valleys.

Yours,
Oscar Lewis, Dublin 2

Lily Murphy replies:

Recently, I travelled with a friend to West Cork, where we did come upon townlands in which the locals had no Irish, and a kind of shame seemed to linger concerning the Famine. 'We hadn't any famine here,' one farmer assured us. 'It was over there, in the next valley.' My friend is a chef, and was eager to explore some of the splendid restaurants of West Cork, and we did eat very well. We had not expected to see *killeens* or to be compelled to think about hunger amid such plenty, and since we were on an eating tour, the irony of coming upon such memorials did not escape us. But we did indeed see them.

This brings me to another of Mr Lewis's points. He is right to challenge me about the nature of my job and my concern with social issues like the Famine and its legacy. I, and others of my profession, could certainly be regarded as hedonists, discussing asparagus or strawberries or cognac as though such things really mattered, focusing only on our palates and bellies in a world where children die for want of bread. Therefore how dare I, a food critic, condemn Hungry Grass for its tactlessness? I would respond that meals can offer us more than pleasure for the senses or satisfaction for the stomach, or an excuse for 'foodies' to indulge their obsession. They can be, after all, a kind of sacrament. In just about every culture, religious ceremonies include breaking bread, or a banquet (or a fast) or a libation for the gods. Nearly all great family occasions, from weddings to funerals, centre on the ritual feast. When Hades ravishes Persephone, spiriting her to the Underworld, she eats a bit of fruit that keeps her at his mercy for part of the year. And during that time, her grieving mother, the goddess of grain, blights the earth so that there is no harvest. Then, when Persephone is released and spring returns, how grateful people are, for the flowering, the fruit, the fattening animals, the corn. Surely we can come to the table with gratitude, and eat our meals with respect for the food, and for the intimacy with others that the breaking of bread and the pouring of wine provide.

I do not intend to sound sanctimonious about all this, but I cannot approve of a restaurant that takes such an arch view of what the absence of food really means. Anyway, if Mr Lewis is still truly interested, I can fulfil my duty by telling him that the best starter at Hungry Grass is the cold antipasto and the best main course the roast pheasant with parsnips. I would keep away from the overlarge and curiously tasteless steaks. The sweets are all right but not distinctive, and the house red is the only bargain among the wines, a robust Chinon which is considerably less expensive than every other bottle on the menu.

★

During her London years, Lily had felt a bit like a character in some modern novel, a clever young woman on her own in the big city. She did not fly to America to see her parents, and only twice did they visit her; stilted meetings since they were uneasy in Europe, and she was uneasy with them.

But mostly she was on her own and to some degree anonymous, something she found useful in a country which really was, she had discovered, as class-bound as people said. Confronting this issue of class, Lily came to rely on two things. First, the use of her pleasant, hard-to-place accent as protective coloration; second, evasion of the matter altogether, through embracing the remnants of what used to be called bohemia. She befriended fellow journalists, painters, poets and eccentric scholars; she drank in louche pubs and extolled offbeat restaurants in her column. She continued to follow Jacob's instructions, playing up the exotic nature of her past without going into too many details about the facts of her previous life. And in this way she managed to glide to the side of the class structure and observe it from without.

Once, after her break-up with Hugo and not long before her move to Ireland, the magazine asked her to review the dining room of the London Arts Club. It was not far from her small Chelsea flat; she had sometimes gone drinking there but had never tried the restaurant so the assignment pleased her. The evening she was to dine there, a colleague rang, an old-fashioned, cigar-smoking journalist called Liam Hurdle.

'Come out for a drink with me,' he commanded in his jovial way. 'I'm just round the corner, in a phone box.'

'Sorry, Liam. I've got to work. But you can come out for a meal with *me*, at the Arts Club.'

He walked up to her door, wearing, as always, the time-honoured reporter's uniform of slightly-grubby-Burberry-with-flaring-collar. And of course he had anchored a newspaper under his arm and was smoking one of his foul-smelling cigars. He really did look the prototypical journalist, with a great boulder of a head, shrewd laughing eyes and a pugilist's broad nose. He was about fifty, and married, though no one at *The Londoner* had ever seen his wife.

'Lucky me,' he announced as they walked along the leafy street. 'A free meal at the Arts Club. They do have the most excellent wines, Lily.'

It was a pleasant-looking place, an old house overhung with vines. You passed through a low door into the vast bar, which in turn gave on a large garden full of venerable trees, and flowers that exhaled a waxy, spicy scent. And since this was early summer there were tables and chairs beneath the boughs, and candles, and laughter and the clinking of glasses. The darkening sky had created a spellbound feeling, so that this garden seemed just a bit enchanted; the women's high voices, the men's low replies, the flickering light of their cigarettes, all slightly more mysterious than if it had been daytime.

She settled at a garden table while Liam got their drinks, two house white wines served in enormous glasses. 'Heavens,' said Lily. 'We had better go slowly. Anyway I had better. Or I'll be too pickled to know what I'm eating.'

'Ah, Lily,' he cried, settling beside her and indicating the people drinking their enormous drinks beneath the trees, which were wreathed with lights. 'Isn't this a truly civilised establishment?'

'You had better not call me Lily,' answered Lily. 'People know the name, and if they alert the chef then my review would be compromised. Call me by another name. Another flower.'

He scowled. 'Rose?'

'Oh, I don't like Rose.'

'Ivy? No. Holly? Too Christmassy. Violet then. You shall be Violet tonight.' They touched glasses.

Suddenly a man's voice spoke from behind Lily's shoulder. 'Perhaps you should call her Mistletoe. Then you could kiss her.'

Liam cried, 'Percy Quinton, you are a cad. Listening to people's conversations.'

Lily heard the scrape of his chair as the man rose and approached their table. 'May I join you, Liam and Violet?' he asked, smiling.

He was tall, with broad shoulders from which the stuff of his shirt fell loosely, so loosely and softly that Lily wondered how one knew that the arms underneath were powerfully muscled. He was fair, his hair as light as her own; his eyes, in the uncertain light, a lovely washed blue. But with that very strong body and those watchful eyes, he was, she decided, dangerous, though she could not say how, or why. It was just something she felt as she regarded him standing there against the trees. 'Please do,' she said, and he settled beside her.

Liam and he exchanged some banter, from which she gathered that he was a sculptor; hence those shoulders and arms, and the powerful, brown hands cradling his wineglass. He looks like a certain kind of animal, she thought, something lithe, a panther or a leopard. Then, *Percy Quinton*, she said to herself, *What a name!*

He told her he had been born in Africa of missionary parents, who had sent him to an English boarding school, after which he had attended art college in London. At one point, in the middle of this narrative, he interrupted himself to observe her narrowly and to say, 'Your looks are quite strange, you know.'

Lily liked this, since she herself considered her face peculiar rather than lovely. 'Yes,' she agreed. 'My looks *are* strange. My character, too.'

'Ah,' replied Percy Quinton. 'We shall have to investigate that. Since I am very interested in strange characters. We shall have to meet soon, to discuss yours.' And the way he smiled at her gave her the same kind of dark thrill she would experience a few years afterwards, under the heavy gaze of Theo Ballsbridge. Only she was younger in London than she would be later on in Dublin, so that this man's languor, his casual strength, his eyes that undressed her in the manner of an old-fashioned seducer in an old-fashioned novel, these things did not alarm her. She was still merely intrigued by how perfect he seemed for the role of Handsome and Dangerous

Rogue: give him a black moustache and he could nearly be the villain of a Victorian melodrama.

Under Liam's cynical regard, they arranged to have drinks the following week. Then Percy left, still teasingly calling her Violet.

In the dining room she said, 'All right, Liam. What?'

'Nothing. What the hell is chermoulah?'

'I think it's a Moroccan version of persillade. Why are you looking at me like that?'

'Like what? May I have the fish cakes with chermoulah? And you could take the cold seafood with garlic mayonnaise, and give me a bit to try, a crab toe or a prawn's head. Wouldn't that be nice, dear Violet?'

She looked about, thinking this place resembled a kind of sublime refectory. There were many small tables, but also a large communal one that could have been a school table except for the immense candelabra standing on its fine wood. The walls were hung with paintings of goat-headed men pursuing nymphs through a forest, which might have looked mawkish in a harsher light, but which shimmered mysteriously in the candle-glow. It was a beautiful room, she decided, dark and shining, rich and strange. Even the Olympians might have consented to dine at the big school table, beneath that picture of Pan and the maidens. She read through the menu and said, 'Let's choose the main course. And stop giving me your sardonic smile.'

'He's a smooth talker, Lily. I mean Violet. But he *is* a cad.'

She hesitated. 'You know, I rather like my solitary life. Only I *am* a bit lonely. And he . . . ' She sighed. 'He is amusing, isn't he?'

'So am I,' Liam answered, tilting back in his chair. His cryptic smile had turned regretful. 'I am amusing, as well.'

'Oh, Liam. You're married. And you work with me. It wouldn't be— '

'I know, I know. Anyway, I'd like to try the duck. May I take the *duck*, Violet, since I can't— '

'Yes, you may,' she replied quickly, 'And let's refrain from obscene rhymes, Liam. If you don't mind.'

Percy Quinton brought her for drinks to the French House. At one of the small back tables, they drank the rather good wine and talked slowly, softly, of themselves and their work.

His voice was deep and warm but he was cold, she thought, there was such coldness in those bleached blue eyes and that tense smile. Yet a heat seemed to course underneath; she could feel it in the way he looked at her and in the indolence of his arm, lifting the wineglass. The top buttons of his shirt were undone, giving her a glimpse of hard brown chest; she thought his skin would be hot to the touch.

As people do who are powerfully drawn to each other, they were beginning to feel separate from their surroundings, as if they were in some bright, charged world of their own. The men and women standing at the counter, with their munching of olives and their inconsequential chatter, did not see how the air was shining, but she and Percy Quinton saw. His every gesture promised; her every fibre understood him, knew what each look and each smile meant. Who was the predator and who the quarry? She did not know, or care. At one point he said, 'I was married once and I shall never marry or even love a woman again. But I want you, Lily. I do want you.' And, 'Yes,' she answered, 'I want you, too,' although she knew he was bad news, a bad bet, that he was all of those old-fashioned things, a bounder, a cad, a seducer-and-forsaker. But it was too late. She had begun the headlong rush and it was too late, now, to stop.

They went to his flat and it was the same but more. It was every cliché, the gasping and clutching, the slow burning kisses; there was his chest, hot as she had suspected, hot to the touch and hot against her cheek. Yet also as she had suspected he was so cool. And slow and deliberate, with that air about him of cool authority. So hot, and so cool, while she shook in his arms, helpless, already in love with him, in love with this creature who would never love her in return.

They saw each other twice more. The first time, he took her to dinner at an underground Greek restaurant in Soho. Its walls were decorated with murals of Grecian temples, poplars and curly-haired shepherds, and its food was more or less indifferent, but the place was not famous for its décor or its food. It was famous for its history of harbouring socialists and communists and bohemians of every hue, for its exuberant waiters and for its strong red wine that came from Cyprus in magnums.

They barely spoke and ate little, though they did take a good deal of the wine. She was exhausted with relief, since she had waited two weeks for his phone call like a lovesick adolescent. At one point he raised his fork, heaped with tarama, and fed her; and the salt flavour, the cream, the roe bursting under her teeth, were lovely. He ate vine leaves with his fingers which gleamed with oil, and nibbled olives, and looked at her the whole time, that cool gaze. Then they returned to his flat and made love until morning, his stern voice issuing commands in her ear, *Don't move. Not yet. Ah, yes, like that . . .*

The next time she emboldened herself to ring him, although she feared that this would displease him, that he would turn his aloofness against her for disturbing his cool world with her clumsiness and heat. But her phone call did not displease him; he accepted her invitation to dinner at her apartment, and once again they drank too much wine and fell into each other's arms and did not sleep until dawn.

Why was she doing this? Why these extremes, living like a maiden in a tower, a virgin in a bower, only to plunge so deeply into something that would inevitably break her heart? It was as if the peril, the smoke smell of impending disaster, were luring her onwards, deeper into the dark wood. And sure enough disaster came.

She received an invitation to the launch of a cookery book by a woman who had come to be regarded as a kind of latter day Elizabeth David. Her recipes for herbaceous dishes, and her treatises on olive oil and Mediterranean wines, were all the rage at present; this current book was her fourth. Lily felt obliged to attend, to support another member of London's food world. So she put on her 'book party clothes', a simple black dress, and black ballerina slippers that she could stand in for hours without getting sore feet. And off she went, to the elegant book shop in Jermyn Street where the launch was taking place.

The shop was really too small for this kind of thing. It was hot and crowded, and the poor author was more or less cornered, trying to sign books, smile at people and balance a glass of wine all at the same time. Lily greeted colleagues, including her editor (also dressed in black) and the food critic of *The Times*. Then she saw Percy, wearing one of those loose, partially unbuttoned shirts that seemed to emphasise his strength. He was standing across the room beside a table of books, drinking from a glass of red wine and talking to a man she vaguely knew, an editor at a small publishing house. Lily looked at him across the room and yearned like a schoolgirl, and like a schoolgirl she was shy. But she gulped some wine for courage, and made her way over to him.

'Lily,' he said easily, and coolly kissed her cheek. He seemed unsurprised to see her, but then this *was* the launch of a food book and he might have expected her to attend: might even have come in hope of meeting her? Why else would a sculptor, with little interest in food, appear at this party for a book on Mediterranean cookery? The other man had disappeared. She said, inanely but because one must say something, 'It's quite a crush in here, isn't it?'

'Too hot,' he murmured, giving her that hot-and-cold look, that bloodless blue look, which made the breath catch in her throat. She swallowed and said, 'We could go elsewhere, if you'd like?'

'I can't, tonight,' he answered, still in that easy, neutral voice, 'I'm not alone.' And he said something else, a polite good-bye probably but she did not hear, and moved past to where a young woman stood before another display of books, a rather glamorous-looking woman with bright auburn hair. Percy Quinton took her arm and said something in her ear, and she laughed and looked at him, and then he laughed as well, while his brown hand moved up and down along her bare white arm. Everybody else was flushed and sweating, jostling one another, gulping their free wine and trying for a bit of literary and/or foodie schmooze. But those two, islanded together, were cool and serene. Lily put her glass carefully down on top of a pile of books and walked out into the street.

A light rain had begun to fall, refreshing after the heat of the book shop. She turned her face up and it dropped like gauze on her cheeks. Then she walked slowly along, staring at the shirts in the shop windows of Jermyn Street. It was the dinner hour and the footpaths were nearly empty. She did not know how long she walked like that, going nowhere, gazing stupidly at the shirts, before Percy's voice spoke behind her. 'Come,' he said. 'Come, now, Lily. Don't be upset.'

She turned. He was smiling his dry smile. She said, 'I wouldn't have expected to see you tonight. At the launch of a cookery book.'

'One goes to book launches. To meet people. That man I was talking to, he edits art books.' He paused. 'I didn't expect to see *you*. But perhaps I should have done, considering the nature of your work. I just didn't think. I'm sorry.'

She said nothing. He extended his hand and she took it automatically. Then he released it and mumbled, 'Well, I had better get back to my friend.'

Still she did not speak, and he made to walk away. But then he stopped and turned, still wearing his typical, watchful smile. 'Lily,' he said softly. 'We had some marvellous sex, didn't we? What more did you expect? It was like one of those good meals you write about. Lovely at the time, but then it's over. What more can you expect?'

'I don't know,' she answered truthfully. She knew that she must look composed enough, standing with the rain beading on her hair. She was not crying or trembling; she must look composed enough. But she felt as if she were falling down a well.

It didn't matter. Or so she told herself. It had just been a mad sex thing, over more or less before it began. How many times? Three, if you did not include that first encounter in the garden of the Arts Club. On the surface, at least, she no longer thought about him. If she was bruised, if she recoiled once more into her shell, it had more to do with Hugo, surely, than with Percy Quinton. Percy had been a kind of incubus, while Hugo had been her boyfriend, with whom she'd had a *relationship*. It was Hugo's behaviour that had spirited her back to her early life, where her mother had wounded her and her father had betrayed her. It was Hugo's need to beguile other women, to flirt outrageously in public, that had made the world of intimate relations seem simply too hard. When she considered her retreat from that world, it was Hugo she remembered, not Percy Quinton whom she had barely known except in some dark, mindless way.

By and by, she could barely recall him, this man in whom she had once wanted to lose herself. Although twice she had the same dream, in which a man's brown hand is gliding up and down a woman's white arm.

A little while later she understood that of course it had to do mainly with his Englishness, with that accent, the thin smile, those sardonic attitudes, all his colonial past.

And if you had to be seduced by a cad, then at least it should be an English cad. Or so she had probably felt, at the time.

★

On an evening in June, Lily brought Nicholas to the restaurant that had become her favourite in Dublin. It was not yet popular and she, selfishly, was loath to write about it. (Although she realised she'd have to do so soon, or else Bartholomew – to whom she had recommended it – would file a review first and declare the place his own discovery.) The proprietor was a rotund Frenchman who favoured Byronic blouses with billowing sleeves, and who kissed his regular guests. The restaurant itself had a tiny kitchen, out of which the chef would emerge cradling potatoes in his hands, to put on your plate if he decided he hadn't served you enough, or with a spoonful of sauce for you to try. The menu was written on a black-board, and changed daily. Late at night the small room became riotous. The customers, who were mainly French, would break into song at their tables, and then the chef might suddenly appear with a great plateau of cheeses or a sup of Armagnac for everyone. The restaurant was called La Chaumière, or the thatched cottage.

One Wednesday night at La Chaumière, while they ate *terrine de fruits de mer en gelee avec mayonnaise maison aux herbes*, followed by *crevettes flambees au cognac*, she kept looking at Nicholas' hands. When she'd first noticed them, their fineness had impressed her most of all, but lately she was intrigued by how they were a living record of his years in kitchens. Cut and burnt, with the blood from plucking pheasants and chopping meat encrusted under the cuti-cles and ground into the palms, they were like the hands of a painter, or perhaps a soldier. She had come to know, with her body as well as her eyes, the position of certain permanent calluses he had grown from anchoring a knife or whisk against those long fingers. There were always almost undetectable bruises just above his wrist bone, from oil spattering out of hot pans and striking him there, on that small expanse of forearm unprotected by a sleeve. She had also grown used to a lovely smell that lingered in his clothes and hair, the vague flour, herb and butter smell of the professional kitchen.

Something else he had given her was a more vivid awareness of the secret life of restaurants. Coming into the Matisse's kitchen with him, standing to the side while he and his assistants cooked, she had learnt that dining rooms are an illusion. Out there, people could be languorous, expansive. They could smooth a linen napkin over their knee, try the wine while a waiter stood to attention; they could talk and laugh, or perhaps quarrel or weep, as full plates were put before them, and discarded plates spirited away. But in a way this was a dream world. The real world was in the bowels of the kitchen, and it was completely different from the atmosphere outside. First of all it was so hot. She wondered how they could bear it in there, hour after hour, amid those ovens, cookers, grills: all that ceaseless fire. And it was astoundingly hectic, since at the Matisse everything was prepared *a la minute*, so when a large order came in, the kitchen was at once galvanised and crazy, with knives flashing and cooks exhorting, but with Nicholas somehow managing to move from oven to counter and back as gracefully as her grandfather had once danced.

Now he said, 'Sylvie rang me yesterday. She's finally managed to get it together. About that party she said she wanted to throw. Next Friday? I can take the night off.'

She smiled, but felt apprehensive. She had decided she liked not only Sylvie, but also the young woman Philippa with her hazel hair and kind hazel eyes. She had even come to like Theo Herbert, despite, or perhaps because of, his surliness. And Bartholomew was very funny in his anachronistic way. It was just that those people were so mannered, even more so than the few aristocratic types she'd met in England. Somehow it made her uneasy. Also she was still at that point of being in love when you don't want other people around. But 'Friday night is fine,' she smiled, and raised her wineglass.

The usual suspects had gathered: Count Bartholomew wearing a Dickensian dress suit with a cravat; tranquil Philippa; Sylvie's husband, Will (fair and smiling in contrast to his saturnine brother); Sylvie herself in a marvellous silver dress that gleamed like fireflies. And there were quite a few others whom Lily did not know, mostly young or youngish except for one beautiful old lady with white hair and large blue eyes. Florid Christopher was not present, she registered with relief.

Nicholas identified people for her: a film director, an angular female playwright and her equally hollow-cheeked poet husband, two members of an Irish traditional music group. 'It should be a good party,' he murmured, 'with this eccentric mix.' But suddenly he stiffened. 'Oh, shit. Over there by the drinks table. Charles Whitby.'

Lily followed his gaze to where a blond man stood laughing. It struck her immediately that he was one of those upper-class men whose face is forever childishly plump with privilege, the cheeks a bit too rosy, the hairstyle a bit too schoolboyish, the clothes also suggesting public schools and playing fields, even as the eyes hardened into middle age. 'Who is he?' she asked softly.

Nicholas sighed. 'A prat. And, unfortunately, a restaurateur. He's the owner of that new Italian in Bray. I've nothing against him, but whenever we stumble into each other he's terrifically unpleasant, perhaps because all his restaurants eventually fail, or because he's originally from the North, too? Anyhow he happens to be one of those people who can really wound. He's not all that bright but he's got an instinct about where other people are vulnerable, and when he moves in for the kill it can be a psychological blood bath. Incidentally his wife is a food critic for one of those women's magazines. I don't really know her but she's always been pretty polite to me. There she is at the window. Maybe you've heard of her? Odile Hackett.'

'Oh! I *have* heard of her.' Odile Hackett was meant to be a good writer, albeit in a workmanlike way. Now Lily regarded her. Her skin was very dark, as though sun-scorched, and she had long coarse hair of an unnatural dead black. Her face was heavy-featured, with shockingly light eyes. She was wearing a nondescript brown jumper and black trousers, and a funny black-and-brown cap. All in all she gave an impression of deliberate duskiness, as though she had cultivated only the most sombre hues, and had perhaps even burnt her face with sun lamps and coloured her hair pitch-black in some curious attempt to attain an ideal of darkness. 'She looks weird but interesting,' Lily whispered, 'In fact she reminds me of Theo – a bit sinister on purpose, if you know what I mean.'

Just then one of the traditional musicians walked over and began explaining to Nicholas that he wanted to throw a surprise birthday party for his daughter at the Restaurant Matisse. Lily moved away, towards a French door that gave on the small garden. She felt somewhat out of her depth, encircled by Sylvie's varied milieu, though it was not an unpleasant sensation; in fact it was nearly restful. She could drink her glass of wine, and eat the lovely hors-d'oeuvres that some good caterer had prepared, and observe the chattering crowd without feeling obliged to plunge in. But presently Theo came up beside her, and once more she was struck by the troubling force of him. That louring gaze, those broad shoulders sheathed in fine cloth, disturbed her strangely. It was sexual, of course, in a Percy Quintonish way, but he also exuded a different kind of challenge, one that caught like a burr in the web of her psyche. Perhaps he did obscurely recall her to her mother, of that old place where love and violence collide. He said, 'So, Lily Murphy, restaurant critic, what is your favourite kind of food?'

'French, I suppose.' She smiled. 'When I was first in France, and I heard the expression *crise de foi*, I thought it meant "crisis of faith".'

He laughed. 'It *is* a crisis of faith, when their livers are sick. Food is a religion, for the French. When you see the women in the markets examining some cheeses or bread, their *concentration*, then you know the French care about food more than anything else. Even more than wine. Or sex.' He gave one of his slow, nearly insolent smiles.

The elderly woman with blue eyes approached, and Theo introduced her as 'Annabel Stuart, my kinswoman.' Touching his arm excitedly, she announced, 'Theo, I have made a decision about what to do with that farm in Wexford. I shall raise llamas.'

'Llamas?' queried Theo and Lily in unison.

She widened her ingenuous eyes. 'They are lovely creatures, kind and peaceful, with the most *adorable* faces. And no doubt mine will be the first llama farm in Ireland. I have always wanted to be first at *something*.'

Lily took another glass of wine proffered by a smiling waiter, and moved away, glad enough to abandon Theo to his cousin and her llamas. But then, to her dismay, she glimpsed Nicholas across the room, talking intently with Charles Whitby. They both looked agitated, the blond man scowling, Nicholas white with emotion. He had put a hand on Whitby's arm, perhaps to console or appease him, but as Lily watched, the other man shook it off. She ventured closer, and realised with a shock that Nicholas was already drunk. While he spoke, he kept listing to the right and left, and his eyes were half closed. Lily heard him say, 'Come now, Charles, come now. This is not *fair*,' while reaching out to seize a fresh tumbler of wine from one of the passing waiters.

Whitby growled, 'It's no good, Savage, and you know it. Everybody who is anybody in this town thinks you're a fraud. Your cooking is just gimmickry, and the Restaurant Matisse – what a twee name! All that kitsch! Absolutely sick-making. You may deceive the middle-class masses who gobble up your pretentious dishes, but you cannot deceive me. Your fancy restaurant is only a cover-up.'

Lily was astonished when Nicholas, instead of getting angry or stalking away, implored, 'Why this bile, Charles? We've known each other for years. What do you have against me?'

She sidled closer. With another shock, she had understood what was going on. Nicholas had stumbled into a place bitterly familiar to herself. As a child, she had petitioned a barren source for mercy, again and again. And how clearly she saw herself in Nicholas now. He really seemed to believe that if he were candid, if he extended a hand to this malicious Whitby, the man would be *moved*, might actually *relent*. When, in reality, he was relishing his power over Nicholas, registering with gleaming eyes that his victim had got drunk and was therefore weaker.

Now he gave a nasty laugh and continued, 'And of course I know your filthy little secret, you Belfast guttersnipe. I know that every night when you put off the lights in your chic dining room and go back into your kitchen to tidy up, you can't wash the blood off those fine hands of yours, can you?'

Lily wouldn't have thought it possible, but Nicholas turned even whiter. Confused, she looked away, out of the open French door at a beautiful twilight, the clouds flushed like a Tiepolo. And suddenly she felt a tremor, an intimation of some sadness, a wistful feeling connected to the dying sun, though of course her heart was breaking for Nicholas. She was preparing to say something, anything, to leaven the tension, when a presence glided up beside her, soft as a shadow.

She turned, and confronted the dark face and pale eyes of Odile Hackett, who spoke with an unwarranted familiarity. 'Lily, I just don't know what to say. I don't know if I can even speak to you anymore.'

Lily stared at her in bafflement. They had never met, yet the woman had addressed her by her first name, and was threatening to end a discourse that had never begun. She continued, 'You shouldn't do it, you know. You're an outsider. You shouldn't come here and offend us with your impertinent reviews. You really do have no shame. And everyone knows you didn't get your job honestly. Nicholas Savage used his connections to advance you. So not only are you an interloper, you're unscrupulous as well.'

Shocked yet again, Lily cried, 'I write for an English magazine. I was a restaurant critic for ten years in London. What does my job have to do with Nicholas?'

She was so astounded, and felt so defiled by this creature, smiling thinly beneath her absurd cap, that she turned and made to flee, but collided with Nicholas, who was standing just behind her and staring glassily into the distance. Charles Whitby had vanished.

'Nicholas!' She clutched his arm. She was still concerned for him after the things Whitby had said; but was feeling so beleaguered herself, she wanted to implore him to defend her.

The woman moved closer, still smiling. Lily had an impression that she was smouldering, as if some dark essence, like char, were literally issuing forth from her. 'Yes, Nicholas,' she said, taking his other arm. 'It's true, isn't it? *You* gave this woman her break in Dublin, didn't you?'

He laughed peculiarly. 'Oh, yeah. 'Course I did. I'm very powerful. All Dublin knows that.'

'Nicholas!' Lily cried again, nearly wailing. 'Nicholas, can't you hear this woman? She's slandering me! Don't *agree* with her!' But he continued to stare over her head in a way that seemed stricken or perhaps merely drunk.

Meantime Odile Hackett, fairly chortling, had curved an arm about his waist. She gave him a light kiss on the cheek. 'Thank you, Nicholas. I knew you wouldn't lie to me.' Her other hand caressed his chest. 'You're a splendid chef. You shouldn't undermine your reputation by letting a little schemer manipulate you. Everyone in Dublin knows a man like you could do *much* better than this talentless thing.'

He favoured her with a lopsided smile. Lily saw he was too drunk to appreciate what had happened. In fact, he probably felt pleased that Odile Hackett was simpering at him since perhaps he could use her coquetry as a means to injure Whitby. She continued to bridle triumphantly, although it was unlikely Nicholas had even heard her. Yet Lily had heard, and it had pitched her into an almost insane distress. The dark potion she had been made to drink just now, composed of a malign woman, a disloyal man, and the corrosive powers of alcohol, was the stuff of her worst dreams, an abrupt return to that suburban house beneath a darkening sky, to the Gorgon and her eunuch, and to herself as the helpless victim. Oh, it was her parents and Hugo and Percy Quinton all rolled into one, though even worse.

She knew she should not appeal to Nicholas now. For some reason Whitby had thrown him into anguish; he was way too upset, as well as drunk, to rescue her. But she was no longer rational. The Hackett woman, still clinging to him, looked monstrous as a harpy to her eyes. A voice inside her was lamenting, like a woman keening, but presently she realised it was no longer internal. She was actually crying, 'Please, oh, please. Can't you hear what's happening? Don't *listen* to her. Please *help* me. Don't *listen* to her . . . '

Odile Hackett said serenely, 'Nicholas, why are we talking to this silly girl? Let's go into another room, shall we?' She lifted her face to his, and once more he smiled blearily at her.

Lily suddenly felt furious. Ignoring Hackett, she shouted at Nicholas, 'How can you do this? How can you listen to the lies of this evil woman? How can you abandon me like this?'

The vague look in his eyes disappeared as his face turned sharp with anger. He shouted back, 'Oh, fuck off. Why are you always bothering me with your insecurity? Leave me the hell alone!' It seemed to her that a faint Northern accent was twanging through his speech now.

Odile Hackett, laughing softly, continued to smooth her

hand in circles over his chest.

Abruptly, Lily felt calm, the dull calm of defeat. The room came back into focus. Everyone was staring at them. She registered Whitby's cruel smile, Theo's narrowed eyes, the look of disapproval on the face of Annabel Stuart. Calm and light-headed, she walked out into the little garden.

Paper lanterns hung from the trees but it was still quite dark. There was a stone wall laced over with vines. She plucked a leaf and crushed it in her palm. Presently she felt someone come up beside her, and turned to see Sylvie's firefly dress glinting faintly. 'I'm sorry, Sylvie,' she said.

She heard Sylvie sigh though she couldn't really see her face. 'My dear Lily, why should *you* be sorry?'

'I screamed like a fishwife in there. I . . . ' She inhaled the garden smell of loam and wet stone. 'I disgraced myself.'

Sylvie was silent a moment. Then, 'Listen. Some of the people in that room are terribly nice. But others are, shall we say, dangerously idle. They are amusing enough, only they haven't enough to *do*, so that someone else's distress is a welcome distraction. They would love to see a proper brawl between you and Nick. Do you see what I mean? Don't give them the satisfaction, Lily. Come back inside with me and have a glass of champagne.'

She complied, though she did not know how she survived the remaining hours of that party. Tactfully, as though nothing had happened, Bartholomew chatted to her about a new Indian restaurant in Parnell Street, and Philippa admired her necklace. There was a stand-up supper, and she managed to swallow some food. At one point she surveyed her image in the bathroom mirror, and was relieved to see she did not look too distraught, except that her eyes

were unnaturally bright. Later she glimpsed Odile Hackett and
Whitby standing in a corner, engaged in a tête-à-tête and eating
from piled plates. She surmised they were never so close as when
they had eviscerated a couple of victims. They had worked up an
unhealthy appetite and were feeding with gusto now. She did not
see Nicholas, and did not care to.

Once more she walked out into the garden. A figure was
slumped on the single bench.

'Nicholas?'

It was too dark to see his face. He muttered, 'That man . . . '
then fell silent.

She waited, and he resumed, 'That man, Whitby, he said he'd
been up to Belfast, on business. Met some people who knew me.
They told him my aunt . . . ' He sighed. She settled beside him. He
spoke again. 'She was my favourite aunt.' Once more he was silent.
Behind the French door, the party was still going strong: a woman
laughed shrilly, and someone turned up the music.

'When I left Belfast I never told her. So she didn't contact me.
Probably believed I wouldn't want to see her. And now she's dead.'
Lily thought she could still detect that faint Northern accent. He
continued, 'Died all alone. And your man Whitby seemed to enjoy
telling me. Accused me of being ashamed of my past. Of not loving anybody. Which is partly true.'

'Oh, Nicholas.' She felt sorry for him, but her own disappointment was still so bitter. She reflected on Whitby's strategy. He had
probably delivered his news brusquely, giving Nicholas no time to
recover before moving in for the kill, accusing him of fraudulence
and cruelty in both love and work, and levelling his accusations so
adroitly, with such focused malice, that his foe had finally collapsed

into the crumpled creature beside her now. She realised that Charles Whitby was Nicholas's *antagonist* in the most literal sense, the true nemesis, who would crush his opponent's spirit. But why such enmity? And why had his wife entered into a dark compact with him? Lily did not consider it unlikely that their two-sided attack had been discussed beforehand. It had been a kind of desolate ballet, Whitby dropping away while Odile glided in, unfurling her black wings. As for Hackett's seductive behaviour towards the man her husband loathed, what did that say about the nature of their marriage? It didn't make a pretty picture.

Nicholas continued, 'And he's right, damn him. He does know my dirty secret.' He fumbled in his shirt pocket for a cigarette but let it drop to the ground. She didn't bother retrieving it for him. He said, 'You don't know, you couldn't possibly know, how loveless that place was. We were all so fucking ignorant . . . '

He fell silent. She wanted to ask what Whitby had meant about Nicholas having blood on his hands, but suddenly she was too tired. 'Let's go, Nick,' she said abruptly. 'Try to walk properly, so it doesn't look like I'm *carrying* you home.' She took his arm and he shambled to his feet. 'Let's go,' she said again. 'All I want is to get away from here.'

They managed to leave without saying goodbye to anyone.

Yet his flat was no refuge. Lily was haunted by his own words accepting Whitby's accusation that he was unable to love. She was punch drunk and drunk in reality, having taken too much wine at the party herself in some forlorn attempt to feel less wretched.

As soon as they were in through the door she turned on him, screaming. She screamed like her mother, spewing every filthy word she knew. It was as though her composed, Lily self had always been a husk, which erupted now, loosing her real self – her volcanic mother self – into the room. All the bitterness she had felt when Odile Hackett used him as an instrument to wound her, all her humiliation, bubbled up like lava; she was rampaging. A small part of herself counselled restraint since their situation was falsified now by drink and high emotion. But despite his entreating voice, and even though she could hear herself screaming, she was unable to stop.

He bowed his head beneath her tirade in a long-suffering way that made her angrier, though it occurred to her that if he would only put his arms round her she might stop. Finally, she did not know when, she was just too exhausted to go on.

Presently he slid into bed beside her but she turned her back to him. In a low and much more sober voice he said, 'Well, you've given them a nice victory, anyway. They got what they probably wanted. A grimy quarrel.'

'*I* did not give them their victory. *You* did. You shouted at me to *fuck off.*'

She heard him sigh. 'I was drunk. I didn't know what I was saying. But you . . . You're letting them wreck us.'

She stiffened: the worst was true. He believed they were wrecked and that she had done it. She had wrecked them on the shoals of her terrible fury. He had seen the real Lily and had recoiled. *Wrecked.* 'No,' she mumbled wearily, without fully understanding what she meant. And then she must have slept.

But at about four in the morning her eyes opened. He was

sprawled beside her, deeply asleep. Yet she was lucid, staring at the ceiling, still as a tomb effigy and feeling as if a part of her had died, loathing Nicholas, loathing herself, rigid with regret.

She slept again, and dreamt that she and Nicholas were travelling in France. They have come to a mysterious farm, apparently unin-habited, all grey stone with a central court.

They enter one of the outbuildings (with the strange logic of dreams, they know where they are going despite never having been there before) and descend a wooden flight into the cellar. It is dark and cool, the walls gleaming with damp. On wooden trestles, great round cheeses are ripening. Their white rinds, stippled with russet and with a texture like flannel, tell her they are brie or camembert. They billow a bit, which means that they are just about ready to be eaten. If she were to cut into one, it would flow like honey from beneath its rind. She and Nicholas move soundlessly through the room, touching the cheeses. They are like treasure in a cave, she thinks, breathing in their rich smell. In the dream she is happy. She turns to Nicholas, but he is no longer there.

When she opened her eyes the room was full of sunlight. Nicholas was in the bathroom; she could hear the shower. On Saturday his restaurant did a big, popular lunch and he would have to get there early. The thought of the Restaurant Matisse crowded with *le tout* Dublin – including people who'd been at Sylvie's party last night – nauseated her. She pressed her face into the pillow. How could he bear it, that dining room full of mindless chatter, the lip-stick-smeared glasses, the half-eaten meals congealing on the plates, the rubble, on each table, of crusts, cigarettes and coffee cups? She pictured him carefully garnishing a dish, and then his Saturday afternoon customers guzzling their lunch distractedly while laughing or crowing, relishing the sauce of gossip far more than his subtle food. Oh, she was still feeling bitter all right, her disaffection deepened by what she had begun to realise was a particularly nasty hangover.

She recalled her dream and her throat thickened. Everyone, she thought, houses their own secret cargo of love, grief and rage. And everyone is alone, for the feeling your beloved has kindled was always there, sleeping inside of you, part of your own solitary source; and the same is true for grieving, and anger. She had believed in love as an everyday miracle because it makes a true connection possible, but now her heart was bleak: *everyone is merely haunted by their own obsessions. The love they feel for another is just part of their own inner world, which no one else can comprehend, not even the beloved himself.*

She pictured a man walking from the dark street into a lighted restaurant, where a motherly *patronne* bustles forward to greet him. She escorts him to a table and serves him attentively, asking does he like the wine? Is the beef done properly? And in that place, encircled by fellow diners, he believes, briefly, that he has overcome his loneliness, conquered the cold night and the dark street. But of course this is an illusion. The other diners barely notice this shy-looking man at his solitary supper. His hostess's warmth is an act, her smile mechanical, and in the kitchen her husband cooks not with affection, but professional indifference. And finally, his meal eaten, the man who believed for an hour that he was receiving real hospitality, is presented with the bill. So much for communion. So much for compassion. The man returns to the road, his stomach full and his wallet lighter, while inside he is already forgotten as the *patronne* replaces his used tablecloth with a fresh one.

Full of such private loneliness, Lily gazed without speaking at Nicholas when he emerged from the bathroom. He muttered something about coffee and disappeared into the kitchen. Sighing, she put on the robe made of white towelling he had given her after they'd first made love, and followed.

Over coffee he said, 'I'm sorry, Lily, but you— '

The anger shuddered through her again. 'You're *sorry*. All you can manage is you're *sorry*? After you let that bitch drape herself over you and say terrible things about me— '

He groaned. 'Jesus, Lily. Must we go over this for the hundredth time?'

'She suggested you go with her into another room. I was sobbing with distress but you *shouted* at me! You told me to *fuck off*, remember?' She was shouting again by this time.

Nicholas gave another groan. 'Oh, stop roaring. I have a killer headache.' He dragged a hand through his hair. 'I didn't know what was going on. I was too upset and I'd had too much to drink. I literally didn't hear Odile say those things. Anyway we went over this endlessly last night, with you shrieking at me.'

She tried to keep her voice even. 'You're reproaching *me*? For raising my *voice* after what was probably the worst evening of my *life*?'

'Lily,' he said. Then he sighed. 'I told you. I didn't hear any of it. I was shell-shocked— '

'Yes, by that man you were *wooing*. Yes! You were! You'd told me he was a nasty prat but then you *appealed* to him; you clasped him by the arm as if he were your *friend*. I don't understand those things he was saying to you and I'm not sure I care, but it was you who *let him in.*'

Nicholas looked away, his face hard. 'I was in no position to help you. I know I said some awful things but I was actually thinking of my own insecurity and pain. I'm sorry.'

She acknowledged he was at least partly right: she shouldn't have beseeched him to protect her as if he were her father. Nicholas was not her father and Lily was not a child: it was about time she learnt how to protect herself.

He muttered, 'Anyway, I've got to prep for lunch.' He rose and dressed while she drank a large glass of water. He was halfway out the door when she said, 'Nicholas.'

He came back into the kitchen; she put her arms around him and started to cry for the first time since their quarrel. After a moment he murmured, 'I'll tell you why, darling. I'll tell you why Whitby upset me so badly. But now I must go.'

After he left she lingered at the table. She thought everything in the room – the bowl of eggs, the strands of garlic, the blue teapot – was almost shining with a kind of pathos. Only she didn't know exactly what she meant by this and presumed her hangover was giving her strange ideas. Automatically she bathed and dressed. She was reviewing a restaurant that afternoon, but had decided to stop at the Arts Club first, to collect her post.

In her room the phone rang.

'How have you survived last night?' asked Sylvie's light voice. 'I'm absolutely *poisoned* from drink. Fourteen glasses of claret was *not* a sensible idea.'

'I hope I didn't ruin your party,' said Lily dully.

There was a pause. 'Nonsense. I'm sorry about that boor Charles Whitby. We only asked him because Will had put some money into his new restaurant. I'd no idea he had it in for Nicky.'

'But it wasn't only Whitby, as you know. You heard me screaming about the terrible wife. First she reviled me, and then manipulated Nicholas, who was drunk and upset, into agreeing with every filthy word she said.'

'Oh, damn. Do you know what the Dublin wags call her? Odious Racket. Or sometimes Odiferous Hatchet. Or else Odile the Hack. I *am* sorry, Lily. Listen, let's have lunch at the Matisse? We can drink a hair of the dog and I can apologise to Nick for last night, and take *you* out to a meal for a change.'

'Thanks, but I'm working. You can come with me though, if you'd like.' She hesitated. 'Nick and I quarrelled last night, after we got home. Those Whitbys were so ruthless, and afterwards we turned on each other. Nicholas said I was letting them wreck us and perhaps I was, perhaps I was. But I was so shocked by Odile Hackett's "motiveless malignancy". And I have always been afraid of calculating women.' She paused a second time. 'We made it up this morning, though I'm still very tired. Anyway, please come out to lunch with me, if you don't mind me being a bit morose.'

In a voice of gentle reproof, Sylvie said, 'Lily, my dear, you needn't ever pretend with me. I am your friend, remember? And I'd love to come out to lunch with you.'

Chapter VI

If I had infinite money, I would live in a hotel. I must admit to a near-loathing of the domestic, of the 'home,' or at least the kind of home in which I grew up: Saturday morning, say, in autumn, the air parched from steam heating. A smell of beds, of the grown-ups in their night clothes (few adults seem to realise that their hairy bodies and feral smell are invariably alarming, if not disgusting, to children).

Another specific memory. This time I know my age: I am twelve. It is the day before Thanksgiving. I am walking home from school. There is a pewter sheen on the clouds, and the air smells of wood smoke and resin. Squirrels scurry up and down the maples while I shuffle through their fallen leaves, swinging my school bag, singing to myself. Tomorrow is a holiday, but my song is bitter-sweet.

Our house smells of butter, apples, cinnamon. My mother is

baking pumpkin and apple pies, savoury pastries like quiche lorraine and vol-au-vent, all for tomorrow's feast. She gives me a glass of milk and a plate of buttery cookies, still warm from the oven. I unravel my scarf, and bashfully tell her about a boy with golden-brown hair, who walked part of the way home with me. His name is Pierre because he has a French mother. I have admired him from afar for a year. 'He walked me to Elm Street,' I say nervously, 'and we talked about lots of things. But then he left, very *fast*, just as we came to Elm Street. He sort of mumbled something, and turned around, and walked off. Just like that. Did I do something wrong?'

My mother says, 'Boys are shy. And when they like a girl it makes them shyer. He probably felt awkward and didn't know what to say. It's good that you had a nice talk. What would you like to wear tomorrow?'

Afternoon deepens into evening. I do homework, while my mother, in the kitchen, alternates between tomorrow's baking and preparations for tonight's dinner. I ask, 'Can I help?' and she says I may wash lettuce and chop garlic. She is painting the top of an apple pie with a wash of egg, pausing to drink from a glass which is full of a blue-white liquid, clear as water yet thicker, so that it furrows slightly against the ice.

Presently my father comes home, wearing his overcoat and scarf, and smelling pungently of the outdoors, a refreshing smell against the effulgence of sugar, butter, roasting meat and gin that has begun to overwhelm the rooms of our house.

It happens over dinner. Suddenly my mother, whose posture is unnaturally stiff and whose neglected food is growing cold on her plate, looks at me with half-closed eyes and mutters, 'A boy— '

'Caroline,' says my father. (Have I mentioned that my mother's name is Caroline?) 'Caroline,' he repeats faintly.

'This *boy*,' she continues, 'this *boy* who walked you *home* . . . '

I am light headed with dread. A boy. That a boy may like me. I take a minute to wonder why I continue to place these confidences, frail as birds, into her hands. Invariably she will wring their necks. But I was shyly proud this afternoon. It was a sort of forgetting. Regarding her then-smiling face, I had chosen not to remember this kind of soiling.

'Do you think a boy would be interested in you? He hurried away because he was ashamed to be seen with you . . . '

'Ah,' says my father, 'leave the girl alone.'

I put down my cutlery and rise. My mother mutters, 'I haven't said you may leave the table, you little shit.'

In a detached way I am interested in her dissolution, the increasing foulness of her tongue. But of course I am not really detached, and because of such scenes, I have never been good at quarrels. I realise some couples actually enjoy a spirited row, but if a friend or lover is angry with me I grow wild. *All is lost*, the small girl screams, while her adversary is taken aback by the extent of her anguish, and indeed her fury. And then, when the din dies down, the fury spent, we gaze at each other, my shouts echoing in our ears. And I will wonder why I plummeted so deep. Once, after an argument, Hugo said, 'Lily, you take these things so seriously. You shouldn't *shout* so. It's as though you thought I would abandon you or something, just because we were angry with each other. Quarrels needn't be so *total*.'

I wonder how I survived. I was an imaginative child: I had books and my rituals for solace. I threw a web of fantasy over my unclean house. I read stories about English schoolchildren, ate those special meals of cheese and olives, made up songs that I sang as I walked home from school, shuffling through the fallen leaves.

Then there was love. How did I come to believe in it? But I did, I do. I believe that you may journey, yet again, into the most terrifying place, and come back. You may find yourself standing in a room, after a row, flushed and trembling. And your beloved is also there, never having left you at all. He made the voyage out with you, and the return as well. You have, after all, come back . . .

★

Lily's friend, Vivian, along with some of the other pupils, had felt oppressed by boarding school. They'd disliked the communal and isolated nature of it, the frumpy uniforms, the tepid showers, iron beds and dour corridors; the meaningless hierarchies and everywhere the high-pitched voices of girls.

But Lily had felt as if she'd been liberated into herself. At home in New York, a certain flame, a spirit-light, had burned and burned in her, unassuaged. She had not been allowed to be herself, for her mother had blundered into her deepest precinct.

Then school had restored her. The building itself was a manor house, made of dark yellow stone, and one evening Lily had regarded Vivian where she stood before a refectory window, with the dying sun limning her profile. And Lily had thought, *There she is; Vivian, outlined in gold; those are the planes and angles of her face: she is herself.* And Lily had extended her own arm into the warm light, and had felt briefly that she, also, was herself.

Their headmistress, Miss Featherstone, often declared that Life would bring her girls their measure of sorrow in due course, and so to impose hardship upon them would be capricious and wicked. In other words, she did not believe a programme of austerity, or futile sacrifice, builds character. Therefore the meals at Lily's school were good, if unimaginative. They had muesli and bacon and eggs for breakfast, shepherd's pie or cold meat and salad in the middle of the day, bread-and-butter at tea-time, and a roast, or a curry (Miss Featherstone had been born in India), in the evening, followed by trifle or ice cream, with sometimes a square of cheddar and biscuits to finish, since Miss Featherstone believed that well-educated young ladies must learn the importance of cheese at the end of a meal.

Lily flourished academically, though she was bad at games. But this didn't matter, since hers was not that kind of school. Also they had Science in the lab of a nearby boys' school, and there were dances as well, so the girls never felt too cloistered (although they did find most of the boys oafish.) In any case, Lily was lucky to escape the usual public school travails: she was not singled out for ridicule or bullying because she was 'new', and her teachers were tolerant and kind.

So, unlike many of her friends, she did not feel incarcerated but the opposite, as if she had been released from prison into the garden of her promise. Yet she still concealed much of her life from the other pupils and the teachers and from Miss Featherstone, and not only because she was following Jacob's advice. Her drunken mother and spineless father and their graceless house were her dark secret. So she was not really free – she was ashamed, and afraid. But of what? She would ask herself this at night, surrounded by rustlings and sighs from neighbouring beds, staring up at the high dark ceiling. Sometimes she seemed to glimpse a shadow, the source of her fear, a daemon or perhaps the Rival. But she had no rivals here. So of what, then, was she afraid?

★

The next evening. Thanksgiving. There are guests and laughter. My mother drinks wine with the others, enough to become tipsy, but not enough to make her rancorously drunk, as when she is alone with my father and me. As usual I sense a tension between her and Jacob; the smiles they exchange are stiff, not really like father and daughter. At one point my grandfather touches my cheek. 'Are you all right, my dear? You look paler than usual.'

Before I can answer we are called to the table, for the ritual feast.

★

'This is *not* a salade niçoise,' announced Sylvie, wrinkling her nose at the plate before her.

'No, it isn't,' Lily agreed, although she was not surprised. She had discovered long ago that it's almost impossible to find a properly made salade niçoise outside of Nice itself. Even in Paris it may arrive with bedraggled green beans or chunks of potato, or even *cold rice*, whereas the genuine version never contains cooked vegetables. It's such a simple thing, Lily had often thought: just good lettuce (preferably mesclun de Nice); ripe tomatoes; peppers; olives; some chopped celery, radish, onion and fennel with perhaps a very thinly sliced artichoke heart; a fresh hard-cooked egg; tuna and anchovies, all dressed with olive oil or an oily vinaigrette. Yet so many places get it wrong. Sylvie's salad looked appealing enough, but there were no peppers, no eggs and no anchovies – a kind of culinary sacrilege – and sure enough those tiresome green beans were draped all over the plate.

Lily's starter, crêpe dijonnaise, also looked quite good, though anything called dijonnaise is meant to include mustard, while her pancake, stuffed with mushrooms in a creamy sauce, was technically a crêpe forestiere. She was beginning to think she had taken Sylvie to a very peculiar place. It called itself French but the chef seemed so muddled about the proper French names for things; on the other hand he was clearly a good cook since their starters were delicious. And their hair of the dog – Campari-sodas followed by a half bottle of Sancerre – was making her feel slightly better.

'I'm so embarrassed,' she confided. 'That appalling scene! Everyone heard, Bartholomew and Philippa and everyone.'

Sylvie laughed. 'You mustn't worry about our lot. I mean the Ascendancy lot, or whatever one calls us.'

Their main courses arrived, and once more the menu had misrepresented them. Lily's espadon florentine should have been prepared with spinach, but there was only a rather delicious-looking piece of swordfish, lightly grilled and accompanied by ratatouille. And Sylvie's tete de veau ravigote came with a peppery sauce that bore no resemblance to a ravigote. Only again the food itself was delicate and good, despite the wrong terms. It was as if the chef were genuine and a fake at the same time.

Sylvie went on, 'My lot are all a bit daft, if you ask me. We haven't a monarchy, you see, the way they have in England, where there are ceremonies and things that give people like us a sense of purpose. My Irish lot are like characters in some storybook that a child has got tired of and thrown into the bin. And because we are so anachronistic, we often behave in a self-indulgent way. A bit of shouting at a party wouldn't have shocked Philippa or Ballsy or anyone, really.' She gave another light laugh. 'It wasn't as if you'd come to blows.'

'Well, we might have done. I might have steamed back inside and clouted Nicholas *and* that bitch, if you hadn't come out to the garden to rescue me. Thank you.'

For the second time that day Sylvie said, 'I'm your friend.' She sighed. 'You needn't keep apologising and thanking me, my dear.'

Perhaps it was the hangover making her sentimental, but Lily's eyes misted. She realised she hadn't had a friend like Sylvie since Vivian.

Also Sylvie's words had compelled her to think about Philippa and Bartholomew, and the other members of Sylvie's milieu whom Lily liked. Now she offered, 'Perhaps it's true, what you say about your class. Only I do find some of you very *bien élevé* and charming. Like Bartholomew with his ornate style, and like you.'

Sylvie was silent a moment, her head tilted. Then she said slowly, 'We *used* to be charming, and occasionally honourable. Even during the Famine when most of our lot were incredibly callous, some behaved splendidly, like Lord Gort. And Lady Gregory was so concerned about her tenants, she actually learnt Irish. But these days when the real aristocrats are rock singers and film stars, we must re-create ourselves, discover some new purpose. The Irish have rejected their landlord class and for good reason. So we must reinvent ourselves, if we're not to become dodos. Or if we don't want to become famous simply for having our names in the gossip columns, the way we used to have them in *The Court Circular*.' She smiled shyly. 'I've been thinking of opening an art gallery.'

They finished their meal and called for coffee. 'Anyway, about that dreadful Odile,' Sylvie said, 'I'm sure she only did those horrid things because she's jealous. You're a better writer than she is as well as being better looking, and your boyfriend is *much* nicer than her frightful husband.' She frowned. 'Though I still don't understand why Nick was so susceptible. I spoke to him briefly while you were in the garden, but he just kept repeating that he couldn't stand Charles Whitby.'

Lily remembered Whitby's snarl: *You can't wash the blood off those fine hands of yours* . . . Though she didn't think she should mention this to Sylvie. What she did say was, 'It seems Whitby knows some of Nick's friends up in Belfast.'

'Well, Whitby's people are from the North. His brother is a barrister in Belfast.'

Lily stiffened. *A barrister*. She considered asking Sylvie if she knew much about Nick's life before he came to Dublin, but stopped herself again. It was to Nicholas she should address such a question, only she was not sure how to broach it.

Walking back to Nicholas' flat through Stephen's Green, Lily remembered a story Bartholomew had told her, about a gay couple, connected to the theatre, who had lived in Dublin generations ago. People had got used to seeing them on their daily stroll through the Green, a sedate old pair, the fact that they were rouged and powdered never seeming to shock anyone even in the more conservative city of that time, perhaps because they were so charming. Yet apparently they would squabble openly at times, right in the middle of the Green, shouting until one or other of them flounced away. But one day the older of the two had confided to Bartholomew, 'You know, although we have the most terrible rows, we always make them up.'

'What is your secret?' the Count had asked, and the old director, tilting his head to one side and raising an admonitory finger, had declared, 'Something I shall recommend to you without hesitation. Never let the sun go down on a quarrel!'

Now Lily let herself into the flat. Nicholas would not be back for hours, but she had her review to write. After she had completed it, she found herself feeling so tired from emotion and hangover and her troubled night that she slid off her shoes and fell asleep on the sofa.

When her eyes opened she knew that she had slept for hours. She'd dreamt of her parents' house, invaded by two burglars dressed in black, although in this dream they are not menacing. They extend a little casket to her, overflowing with jewels. One of the men says, 'We are taking this box, but you may keep something, some trinket, for a talisman.'

She stood up, pushing aside the blanket that a thoughtful Nicholas must have smoothed over her. It was dark outside and dark within, although a light was burning in the kitchen.

She found him there at the table, a half-glass of wine at his elbow. He was gazing down at a photograph, but as she approached he looked up with a weary smile. 'Hello, Lilliput. I'm so sorry about last night.'

She kissed his nape, as she was wont to do, breathing in his now familiar chef de cuisine smells of butter, thyme and garlic. 'I'm sorry, also.' She settled in the chair next to him. 'Perhaps we're too babyish, you and I. I go around thinking you should defend me against difficult people. And you think that if I'm troubled, it's meant as a reproach to you. As though we expect our partner to protect us all the time, instead of just being ourselves.'

He squeezed her hand. 'Let me give you some nice Beaujolais. Here, look at this picture.' He rose and brought over the bottle and another glass, while she examined the photo. It showed a little black-and-white Nicholas, four or five years old, standing on a lawn next to a tall woman, her dark hair drawn back, and with some-thing of Nicholas' elegance in the lines of her face. But she wears an ugly dress, patterned with large flowers. She does not touch the lit-tle boy, and neither of them is smiling.

'In my family it would be different', Lily said. 'The mother would be clasping the child tightly. But such a fierce embrace wouldn't make the child feel protected. Everyone was so demon-strative in my family, only it didn't mean they were feeling things *genuinely*.'

Nicholas lit a cigarette. 'I always say to myself how nice it is, that our pasts seem to connect in some way, even though our back-grounds couldn't be more different. Your people were demonstra-tive while mine were dour, but somehow it comes to nearly the same thing.'

They were silent, drinking their wine. Then he gave a soft laugh. 'Have I ever told you about my recurring nightmare? I don't mean a nightmarish idea; I mean a real dream, which I continue to have from time to time. In this dream I'm in the kitchen of the Matisse. Everything is as it should be: the stations ready for service, the grill and ovens fired up, knives gleaming. I can even smell the nice cottony smell of fresh tea towels. Only someone comes in (I never know who it is) and tells me from now on I am obliged to cook the same kind of food I ate as a boy in Belfast. The restaurant has changed its menu and from this day onwards will be serving only fried eggs and chips, and fish and chips, and bangers and chips.'

He clasped her hand on the table. 'I cannot tell you how much this dream disturbs me. I'm like you. I wanted escape, and the means of escape, for me, was food. The meals I cook at the Matisse, the dishes full of fresh herbs, the perfect béarnaise, the organic eggs and meat, these things are a source for me. A source of grace.'

'Ah, I know what you mean. Grace in two senses. Grace like a blessing, a sacrament. And grace as in graciousness.'

'And in the dream I'm exiled from all that grace and graciousness, from fine oils and spices, from Normandy butter and wild strawberries, from good wine. Exiled from the life I made for myself through prayer and desire. Exiled from you.'

Once again she saw how tired he was, with plum-coloured shadows under his eyes. He was explaining, 'I don't have a deep-fat fryer in the restaurant. I loathe deep-fried food, even real pommes frites. And in fact I think the people who know about such things have decided it's actually bad for our health. Heating oil at such high temperatures curdles it or something. And I've already told you that when I was small I couldn't stand the acrid smell of my mother's cooking. For me it was the very smell of loneliness. But in my nightmare there it is, one of those deep-frying machines, right in the middle of *my kitchen*.'

Lily smiled, thinking he was quite the temperamental chef. She had already learnt some of the other culinary things he hated: fish knives; sauces thickened with flour; the waiter pouring out your wine instead of letting you measure your own flagon; the waiter showering black pepper over your food from one of those enormous pepper grinders; the waiter saying 'No problem' when you ask for the bill; customers who ask for their sauce 'on the side'; monkfish, which he thought was 'like eating a fist'.

She touched his cheek, and suddenly she had an impression that there was another presence in the room, as real as the bowl of eggs on the counter, or the fridge which had just made one of its shuddering sounds before falling silent again. She couldn't say what this feeling meant, only that the air seemed alive or shining somehow. Nicholas said, 'I haven't told you everything. I haven't told you what it really meant, to be a little kid in a Loyalist district in the North.'

She tilted towards him to listen more closely. He continued in a low voice, 'I was like them, Lily, I was one of them. I had been brought up to believe that Catholics were evil, and, God help me, I did believe it. We used to go to their estates and scrawl filthy things on their houses: *Fuck the Pope* or *Taigs Out*. Stupid things. We would torment kids on their way to school. Many of my friends became, you know, the real thing, paramilitaries. You know what I mean. If I hadn't got my scholarship, gone off to a good school and met boys like Jonah Chen, it might've happened to me, too.'

In an even softer voice he said, 'Once, when I was about twelve, we accosted a woman, a young Catholic woman with yellow hair, carrying a string bag. She was an ordinary woman, perhaps newly married, maybe even pregnant, with her shopping in that bag for the evening meal. Some of the boys threw the food on the footpath and desecrated it, stomped on it and peed on it. Highly imaginative, weren't we? And then we pushed her up against a wall and . . . ' He gave his dry laugh. 'If an RUC man hadn't walked round the corner at that moment, who can say? Anyway, we scattered, so I'll never know what I might have been capable of, that afternoon. It haunts me, though. I'm still deeply ashamed. I haven't told anyone until now. It's one of the darkest moments in my past.'

She took a deep breath. The last thing she wanted was to invoke last night, and it didn't seem possible that Nicholas could ever have been what he had just described as 'the real thing'. After all, she told herself with a kind of grim flippancy, he hadn't any tattoos. Nevertheless she asked, 'What did Whitby mean, Nick, about you having blood on your hands?'

He looked up at her; then down at the table. 'Not me,' he muttered. 'Not me. My brother.'

She realised she was still feeling that presence, like a light in the room. He said gruffly, 'Are you sorry now, to have got involved with someone from such a lowlife background?'

Cradling his hands, bruised and scalded, in her own, she answered slowly, 'We are alike in another way; we're too afraid of our bad sides. What do you think I'll do, now that you've told me this? Do you think I'll abandon you? You were so brave to escape that life!'

He poured them more wine. Then he surprised her by asking, 'Are you hungry?'

She considered. 'Why, yes, actually.'

He looked round the kitchen. 'I could make avocado vinaigrette, and an omelette?'

She smiled. 'We have just enough wine for it.'

Over the meal he told her more. His parents had been stern, in the manner of their place and time, but not really harsh. In fact they had feared the brutality that was eating like a canker at their city and had wanted both of their sons to flourish in the outside world. 'Oh, they were sectarian all right, and ignorant, but not half as bad as some. So it was weird about Martin. We were all ruffians of course, but he was worse . . . '

Lily didn't know much about extreme Loyalist groups in the North but had read enough on the Shankill Butchers to make her nearly afraid to learn more. 'He was all right as a small boy,' Nicholas went on. 'But then he changed. It began with girls. He was a right bastard with them. He never made love or even had sex. He just *fucked*. He fucked this one and that one, and then he humiliated them in public; really ugly stuff. He seemed to hate people, hate the world. There was no kindness in him.' Abruptly he asked, 'Is this omelette *baveuse* enough?'

'It's fine, Nicholas. Just go on.'

'He joined one of those illegal groups beginning with the letter 'U'. If you ask me, they're the same, the groups beginning with 'U' and those on the other side that begin with 'I', both sides insular and obstinate and mad.' He halted for a moment. 'I'm not sure I can go on now. I mean I've other things to tell you, about my family and myself, but I don't think I'm able for it yet.'

Lily knew how the possibility of finally uttering some home truth can make the breath ragged with fear. She remembered the darkness of his car after their day in Roundwood, how she had spoken almost candidly then. She knew she must wait now.

She said, 'I understand; you will tell me when you're ready. Anyway, whatever he's done, you don't ever go to see your brother, do you, or any of your family? You wanted to be entirely free of that place? Which is why you didn't know your aunt was dead?'

'I went to the funerals of my parents. They both died before their time, not because of the Troubles, or not directly anyway. I'd say the life up there kills people in more subtle ways than just bomb blasts. They were never healthy after Martin changed.' He sighed. 'But you're right. After they died I didn't go back, never called on family or on old friends. So Whitby could really strike where it hurt, at the source of my shame.'

'I'm ashamed, too. I was ashamed of my mother and so I made up stories about my life, but then I was ashamed of lying. Sometimes I think my whole life has been a tangle of shame and lies and then more shame.'

'Not here,' he said, 'not with me.'

Lily remembered how that very morning she had sensed a light in this kitchen, as if homely things like the teapot and the milk jug had somehow begun to glow with what she had thought of then as 'pathos'. And now here she was, still feeling that light, like a third presence in the room.

She moved over onto his knee and kissed him on the mouth; then pushed his hair away to kiss his ear and throat.

Chapter VII

Asian Fusion
Temple Bar
by Lily Murphy

A razor-thin lady at the next table touches her friend's arm and, *sotto voce*, says, 'Aubergines are the new courgettes.'

'I *know*,' replies the other lady, also in a hushed, nearly reverent voice, 'And frisee is very now.'

First of all, I was marvelling that I could hear them so clearly. The acoustics at Asian Fusion are astonishingly awkward: your waiter, reciting the dishes of the day, sounds as if he's under water, whereas conversations across the room are clear as glass. Second, I wanted in all candour to ask the two ladies, 'How can you possibly like frisee?' (Frisee is that spiny, frilled lettuce; nearly impossible to eat because the bristling leaves flop about the plate no matter how hard you try to control them.)

Though of course the two women should not have surprised me. After all, Asian Fusion is the kind of restaurant just such stylishly thin ladies frequent, in order to eat salmon-and-daikon-salad, drink appallingly expensive mineral water and make pronouncements like 'Curly parsley is out,' as if, Heaven forbid, Dublin had been transformed into California.

Asian fusion is a 'now' idea, all right. At its best, in restaurants from Hong Kong to Sydney to San Francisco, this kind of food is dazzling. But, alas, something has gone wrong at the restaurant whose very name is an homage to fusion cookery.

My starter at lunch, smoked trout with wasabi mayonnaise, was weirdly flavourless. The mayonnaise itself was good; rich with egg yolks, obviously homemade. And the Japanese horseradish called wasabi had given it a nice pale green colour – but it did not taste of wasabi *at all*. Not a bit of that head-clearing, nose-prickling, eye-smarting flavour could I detect in the mayonnaise arranged so prettily, in green ribbons, on my plate. As for the smoked trout, its colour was a strident orange and its flavour no better than wan. My companion's first course, a small pizza of duck sausage and rosemary, was more lively, although the crust was too thick. But, then, outside Italy one almost never gets that perfect thing: good ingredients on a crust so delicate it is closer to pastry than bread.

My main course of raw fish (sashimi) with three sauces

was vividly fresh, but my companion's 'lacquer steak' with Chinese mushrooms was overcooked, and the 'lacquer' just a gloss of soya sauce.

The dinner menu is much more expensive, but some of the dishes are splendid, especially the starter of asparagus dressed with truffle oil and the scallops in brandy and ginger sauce. Yet the sushi is simply bad.

Of course, the fish in sushi has to be absolutely fresh, but that isn't enough. All the ingredients, in every morsel, must be perfect or it doesn't work. For the uninitiated, nigiri sushi refers to the bits of raw fish which recline like odalisques on a mattress of seasoned rice. Maki, or rolls, are the bracelets of dried seaweed encircling the same kind of rice, with fish or pickled vegetables faceted in the centre. In both these types, the rice must be moist, the seaweed tender, the whole bundle so compact that it doesn't crumble if you break it in half. Speaking of which, each parcel of sushi should be small enough to pop whole into your mouth. If the pieces are served as big clumsy planks it becomes very awkward – as though handling chopsticks isn't difficult enough for most of us Celtic tigers! Suffice it to say that the sushi at Asian Fusion is cut too large, the seaweed on the rolls is so tough, it's like trying to eat paper, and the rice is dry and crumbly. A real disappointment, especially considering the astronomical cost of one starter-size plate.

On to the main courses, which generally consist of those now-standard Asian fusion dishes that sound exotic yet are too often poorly executed and come across as merely odd: the prawns with rocket and pickled ginger were tough, the beef with Chinese cabbage too salty, the duck with oriental cucumber curiously watery. And *then* there are some weird, ill conceived plates that make you wonder what the chef was taking when he designed the menu. Steak with redcurrant jam! (*Why?*) Tuscan lamb with anchovies! (Really, I'm telling the truth. And don't ask me what makes it Tuscan.) Salmon tartare with artichoke bottoms and fruit salsa! (Yuck.) Lamb's liver with a meringue of peas and mushrooms! (A meringue of peas and mushrooms?)

What culinary hubris! Does the chef here really believe he is creating delicious meals merely by throwing unexpected ingredients together? After all, very seldom throughout history has *anyone* invented a genuine masterpiece, a new dish that actually makes it into the food canon. To offer what might seem a whimsical analogy: Must every novelist defy the boundaries of form, like Joyce, or is it not okay to write a good, even daring novel within an enduring tradition? By the same token, must every chef in the country put curry paste in the ice cream or sea urchins in the mash in order to be 'creative?'

Americans abroad often marvel, 'How do the French eat so much foie gras and camembert, and drink so much wine, and still stay so healthy?' Or, 'How is it that the Italians manage to look so willowy and elegant on their diet of pasta and pizza?' And in the next breath they will exclaim, 'The Europeans are so *rigid* about food, with their emphasis on ceremony, and the proper order of courses, and table manners.' It never seems to occur to such people that the secret lies in the very 'rigidity' which they decry. Perhaps the

French and Italians simply *know how to eat*, how to balance a meal and measure their glasses, because their cuisines have evolved over hundreds of years. It seems to me that to play around with such knowledge, to throw fennel into a dish because fennel is popular now, or to splash soya sauce over fried eggs to make them 'Asian', is simply silly. The few chefs who do succeed at fusion cookery generally have a foundation in classical cooking, and know what they are experimenting with.

Incidentally, the décor here is breathtakingly narcissistic. The no-colour walls are actually decorated with photographs of the façade, bar and dining room, a paean to the restaurant within the restaurant. Actually, the nicest thing about Asian Fusion is the late-night clientele. After about eleven o'clock, a hip, largely gay crowd throngs the bar and tables, an ebullient and colourful antidote to those beige walls.

★

Early in her adolescence, when she was still living in America, Lily had begun to fashion her own private prayers, or gestures, like a particular way of arranging the food on her plate or the books on her desk. She had been reluctant to feel an adult need and an adult yearning. She had fathomed that we are to some degree defined by what we long for, and also that we have partly attained it through the longing itself, because we have already conceived it, it exists in us, through the force of our desire. And she was afraid to feel the kind of longing that would be the measure of her power. So she surrounded herself with incantations and rituals, and in this way protected herself from passion and the pain of loss.

In accordance with her father's family tradition, and because her mother did not object, she had been baptised a Catholic, although her father's parents died when she was very small, and her father himself seldom went to church. But at her English boarding school she attended chapel along with the other girls, and grew to love the solemn beauty of the Liturgy. She still continued with her private prayers, thinking of them as attempts to *appease the gods*, as opposed to the worship of God which she engaged in every Sunday.

At twenty, for the first time in her life, Lily was neither student nor ingénue, but a young woman who took the bus every weekday to her job as an editorial assistant at *The Londoner* magazine, along with other women and men wearing similar serious clothes and travelling to serious jobs. By and by she showed her mettle and was promoted to restaurant critic, and then she met Hugo, and early one summer they went on a holiday to Italy.

They went to Liguria, where Lily had been once before as a child, with her parents, to visit the birthplace of her father's grand-mother. She had been haunted by it ever since, had remembered fishermen spreading their nets over a pearl-grey sea at dawn, and mountain villages where the weather-beaten houses had seemed to list and pitch as they climbed up the slopes. When she returned to Liguria with Hugo, the mountain villages were still there, but the beaches were full of tourists and ice cream, with no fishermen that she could see, although she looked for them.

They stayed in a small town, in an apricot-coloured hotel. Their room was immense, with yellow walls, a very high, wide sagging bed and a balcony. Each morning, in the white dining room, they ate an enormous breakfast of soft-boiled eggs, crusty bread and sweet butter, cold meat and cheese, and fresh peaches and figs, with which they drank cup after cup of the mysteriously delicious Italian coffee. They would look speculatively at the other hotel guests who were mainly older than they, and mainly Italian. Their Italianness pleased Lily, who had come to positively dislike Anglophone tourists, even though she was quite aware of being an Anglophone tourist herself. But the English-speakers – especially the Americans – whom she and Hugo observed at their hotel seemed always to be insisting on their own assumptions, to actually resist the experience of this old and lovely world, to look at it suspiciously while lumbering along the streets, their waists bound with silly money pouches as if any foreigner was a potential thief. Or else to fall in love with Italy in a way that struck her as disingenuous: 'Wow, look at those palm trees! Wow, look at that church!', especially since they patently did not wish to engage with the country on its own terms but preferred to take over the cafés, shops and the beach, talking in loud voices as if they were back home.

One morning over breakfast, Lily noticed a young American couple who were making no effort to speak Italian to the waiter, not even a *buon giorno* or a *grazie*, and then complained to each other about his poor English. After this couple had left the breakfast room, Lily found herself complaining in turn – about them, their arrogance and terrible manners. Then she paused and said, 'Am I being too harsh?'

'Probably,' answered Hugo, smiling mildly. 'But it's understandable. You were born in America; so they made you feel ashamed.'

Lily sighed. 'Only isn't that a narcissistic attitude, or something? They make me feel uncomfortable about myself so I say baleful things about them. After all, it isn't *their* fault I identify with them, is it?'

'Well, they *were* pretty terrible. I'm not used to Americans behaving like that in Europe.'

She looked at him with amused affection, thinking of course he wouldn't be used to Americans behaving like that in Europe, since his Europe had always been a world of privilege, of sumptuous dining rooms, grand hotels, and the Swiss finishing school his sisters had attended. She had met his father, who could be officious, and his mother and sisters, who had seemed fairly frivolous, but they had all grown up with nannies and governesses and French au pairs, had mastered languages and had travelled the world in style. They would never have come across the kind of American tourist who asked if it was safe to drink the water from Italian taps.

Hugo knew almost nothing of Lily's background, because she volunteered almost nothing, and his English reticence forbade him to ask. But she knew he presumed she was from a 'good' family, because she had been at a 'good' school.

As a child and adolescent, she had not known much about how most men and women regarded the world. At boarding school she'd been drawn to certain girls on the basis of their intelligence and charm, failing to realise that many of her fellow pupils, who had grown up discussing Burke's Peerage and who would 'come out' at provincial balls, defined people in terms of background and wealth. Such an attitude would have struck her as offensive, the polar opposite of the ideals her school was meant to cherish, and she wouldn't have credited it; would, in fact, have bristled defensively at something she could not grasp since she had distilled her ideas about society, about manners and morals, from books, and she often spoke like a nineteenth- or early twentieth-century novel, without the colloquialisms of her time and place. People sometimes thought she was from a European country. In fact this was another reason people like Hugo forgave or overlooked her occasional failure to hold a particular fork in a particular way or to utter the correct form of greeting: she had been given a special dispensation as a rather exotic, eccentric and oddly beautiful foreigner, the nature of whose foreignness couldn't quite be labelled.

In their Ligurian town, Lily and Hugo moved away from the tourists through their love of bars. Most of their fellow hotel guests wouldn't have dreamt of climbing up to the Old Town for drinks at the small café Lily and Hugo had discovered, in which elderly ladies drank cappuccinos after Mass, and children played under the tables, and young men clustered at the flipper machine. Neither Lily nor Hugo drank very much, but they relished the bar for the people they found there, whereas the other guests were mainly on full or half board, as if fearing to venture beyond the pleasant dining room of the hotel with its competent staff.

At their favourite bar, they would gaze out of the open door at the smoke-blue dusk, and at the house opposite: peach-coloured, green-shuttered, and with a petite Madonna standing in a recess above the lintel. Cats moved lightly down the street, making no sound.

Along with their Campari-sodas, they were served plates of salami, raw ham, olives and chunks of parmesan as a matter of course. And afterwards they went to one or other of the Old Town restaurants to eat things like a particularly thick macaroni cooked al dente and filmed with pesto or a sauce of cream and walnuts, followed by a fish of the region, orata or branzino, done on the grill or in the oven and served with buttery spinach or planks of roast aubergine. They drank the white wine of the place and spoke of Italy but also of England and America, how in England class was determined mainly by provenance whereas in America it was largely money; they wondered who Henry James would find to write about if he were an expatriate American novelist living in Europe *these* days.

They seldom spoke about themselves, even though they were in love at the time.

★

Spring ripened into summer. One day Lily looked in the mirror and saw that her hair had grown long and flat. So she had another haircut, which, she thought, did not suit her as well as the previous one, though Nicholas assured her it was fine. But she went back to the terse hairdresser, whom she liked, to tell him it was not quite right.

Examining the work he had wrought upon her head, he concluded, 'No, this cut is fine; technically it's the same as the first one. It's only that your hair is thinning a bit. It happens to some women, you know, not only to men. You've lost some at the crown and on the top, so the cut falls differently.'

'I am mortal, after all,' she declared to Nicholas later that day. 'I'm losing my hair. I'm getting *old*.' She was trying to make light of it, but was actually quite upset. The prospect of thinning hair not only alarmed her, it made her feel vaguely humiliated. She pictured the boiled-egg skulls of old ladies, insufficiently camouflaged by feathers of dry hair, looking so naked – almost indecent.

Nicholas said, 'Your haircut is lovely. I don't see any difference at all. Let's go to Lucien's party on Friday. It may cheer you up.'

They found each other exchanging a long look then. The idea of a party was still charged for them. But Lily decided it might be a good idea; might exorcise the still-acrid memory of Sylvie's party. And she liked Lucien, a French photographer who had lived in Dublin for years. He adored Nicholas's cooking and gradually they had become friends. He was a dark-haired, shy gay man, with a nice boyfriend called Didier, also French. 'All right, Nick. Let's give it a whirl.'

It was a dinner party with good simple food (Lucien and Didier had said they were too daunted to try anything really elaborate with Nicholas at their table). So they had made warm goat's cheese salad, and pot au feu, and then blackberries with crème fraiche. There were ten guests, a varied crowd. Lily was placed next to a middle-aged man called Jason, who had taken early retirement from his job at a Boston insurance company so that he and Doris, his wife, could move to Ireland. With a slightly aggressive smile, he told her he had been a 'secret journalist' for years, writing longish essays on American culture. Lowering his voice, he said that he harboured an ambition to publish these pieces in an Irish newspaper, perhaps as a weekly column bearing his name and photograph. Lucien had mentioned that she, Lily, was a journalist. Did she have any promising contacts? Could she help him? Promote him?

Lily stared at him, a plumpish man with round eyes that shone earnestly. He had never grown up, she guessed, was full of boyish enthusiasms and boyish dreams, unaware that such attitudes were not endearing in an adult. She knew she should handle him delicately, explain that it was hard to break into the world of journalism, that only the most seasoned and talented were given weekly columns with their by-line and photograph in a national newspaper. But she feared that if she spoke she would answer him too brusquely. His blend of arrogance and naiveté was exasperating her more than it should have done, perhaps because that revelation about her thinning hair had disturbed her more than she'd thought it would.

Strange how it made her feel vulnerable, as if the cold finger of mortality had touched her newly shorn nape. It was the first time her feminine vanity had been wounded in this way. Despite her insecurity about it, she realised now that she had always relied on her beauty. She'd grown used to double-takes in restaurants, to murmurs rippling behind her as she passed through a crowd. Now she had to consider how her life would change when her beauty diminished. It had always had a lunar quality: night-black eyes and the abundant moon-bright hair. But perhaps that hair would continue to fall out? Perhaps her moon was waning? And now, suddenly, this importunate man, grinning fatuously and pelting her with questions he had no right to ask: tonight she had no patience for him.

Recently, Sylvie had introduced her to an old friend, an elderly priest with a kind face. Over drinks at the Shelbourne, he had spoken about the slow, wrenching decline of Catholicism in Ireland. 'Maybe we deserve it,' he'd said ruefully, 'but it would be a pity to lose some of the nicer points of theology, the instructive things, like our teaching on Presumption, which is defined as "the foolish expectation of salvation without making use of the necessary means to obtain it". I think it can apply to many things in life, to how certain people expect instant success without wishing to work for it, that kind of thing.'

Indeed, she thought now, observing this Jason, who was still giving her an over-eager smile and asking, 'Do journalists have agents? Could you recommend me to yours? I do think my pieces are really first class. Would you like to see them? How about if I submitted some to your editor in London?'

She glanced round the table, hoping Nicholas, or someone, would rescue her, and at that moment Doris, Jason's scrubbed-looking wife, said, 'Well, the Jews are the real problem, aren't they?'

She had been placed directly across from Lily, next to Nicholas, who was lighting a cigarette in his usual way, curving a hand over the flame and frowning. Lily loved that scowl of concentration, was used to seeing it whenever he gazed down at a pot or saucepan, a frond of hair falling across his cheek while he poured cream into a sauce or sprinkled herbs into a casserole. Or when he made love to her, that same frown, the same fall of hair across his cheek.

'Whatever do you mean?' asked Nicholas, looking neither at Doris nor Lily, but only down at his cigarette.

Another guest, a bearded middle-aged solicitor named Tom, said emphatically, 'Of course it's the *American* Jews.' He brandished his wineglass in Doris's direction. 'I mean, don't get me wrong. I admire the Jews. They're intelligent and competitive, though I don't see why they need to be so competitive *the whole time*. Anyway, let's face it, they control everything in America. I mean *everything* – the media, the money, those appalling ultra-conservative foreign policies.'

'Yeah,' said Doris. 'They've been controlling the money for five hundred years.' She chuckled. 'They always change their names, but *we* know who they are.'

Lucien, who had been serving coffee, now settled back in his chair and spoke quietly, 'This conversation is beginning to sound like a dinner table in Berlin, in 1929. People would have been saying the same things then, how the Jews control the banks and the newspapers.' He laughed bleakly. 'If this conspiracy of Jews had really been so powerful, how was it they could not save themselves from the gas chambers? And how do you allow yourselves to discuss them in this way, in this day and age, after all that has happened in Europe? Have you learnt nothing?'

'Hang on, Lucien, don't get me wrong,' answered the solicitor. Lily observed that he had just admonished Doris, also, to not 'get me wrong'. 'Don't confuse me with those neo-fascists who insist the Holocaust never happened. It's the Zionists I'm talking about, those territorial fanatics who believe they have a mandate from God to kill Palestinians. And don't tell me those warmongering zealots in Israel aren't getting help from the American Jews!' Once more he waved his glass in the air, spattering wine on the tablecloth.

Lily reflected that while some of his words offended her, she did not entirely disagree with him. She could understand the Jewish yearning for a homeland since, over so many European centuries, the 'Jew' had been regarded as a dangerous outsider, an avaricious shopkeeper or an unsavoury man in black sidling along a dank passage. So after six or seven million Jews had died in the camps, it seemed natural that the survivors should cry 'Enough! Enough of exile and betrayal: we will go back to our home!' She remembered how the chaplain at her English school, an enlightened man who'd encouraged the girls to study Roman Catholicism and Buddhism and Judaism, had once recited a Jewish prayer full of yearning: *Next year in Jerusalem . . .*

Only it seemed to her that this Jerusalem needn't be made of mortar and stone; surely there could be a Jerusalem of the heart? Surely one's source, one's home, lay in the imagination and the spirit, and in the capacity to love. On the other hand, if certain Jews did wish to live in their ancestral homeland, was it necessary to establish a *religious* state? Couldn't Israelis live side by side with their Palestinian neighbours in a bi-national and secular country? Lily reflected on these things, but said nothing.

Doris spoke up again. She was a large-boned woman, with extruding eyes that conveyed a sense of urgency, as if at any moment they might pop out of her head with emotion. 'I'm sorry, Lucien, but that's *exactly* how the Jews manipulate us. If you criticise them, they say, "Oh you awful Christians. You've learned nothing from the Holocaust." You can't utter a *word* against the Jews these days without them trying to make you feel guilty. It's like, they can do whatever they want to the Palestinians and all, because ever since World War Two, we've been living in Jew-time. I mean it.' She looked round the table with the same earnest expression as her husband. 'I really mean it, you guys. We're living in *Jew-time.*'

Lily realised then something she should have understood long ago. The suburban house that she'd always hated was for her mother a solace and a refuge. For Lily's mother, the streets of Europe (ancient houses, late-night cafés pouring butter-coloured light onto the cobbles outside, the clang of church bells), for Lily's mother such images were full not of romance but menace. She was haunted by her European ancestors who had listened at night to the tread of soldiers in the streets below, who had huddled in railway stations, who had literally gone up in smoke. Therefore she *liked* the uniformity of America; she liked her house which was identical to every other house on its street. She liked it precisely *because* it was barren of memory. Only she was not so safe after all, not when there were Americans like this Doris, who seemed unable to distinguish between Israeli policies and Jews in general.

Throughout the meal, Didier had been so absorbed in serving, clearing and pouring that Lily hadn't been sure he was following this conversation which had arrested everyone else at the table. But now, tilting back in his chair with a cigarette in one hand and a glass of cognac in the other, he said in his charming accent, 'First, my dear Doris, I would like to tell you that I find your words highly offensive, because I am Jewish.'

Lily was pleased to see Doris stiffen and turn red. She made to answer but Didier went on in a firm voice. 'You speak of American Zionists, and of the Zionists of Israel. And I believe you are right, Doris. I believe that there is indeed an alliance between American Zionist groups and the religious fundamentalists of Israel.' He paused and once more Doris tried to speak. But Didier looked steadily into her protuberant eyes until she lowered them. Then he turned to the bearded solicitor who seemed to be drinking an inordinate amount of red wine. 'And you, Tom, you are also partly right. Yet there is one mistake the two of you are making, a crucial mistake which betrays that you are not merely anti-Zionist but in fact anti-Semitic.'

Didier halted to swallow some cognac. The table remained silent. He continued, 'I do not wish to insult the Americans at my table this evening. But I do truly think Americans are different from any other peoples of the West. They are different because they are brought up to believe that they are the greatest country in the world, God's Own Country. And many do believe it. Many sober, good-hearted, Christian Americans believe their lives exemplify freedom and every moral truth, simply because they are American.'

Jason said peevishly, 'Don't generalise, Didier. And I can't see what this has to do with Israel.'

'It ill becomes you to tell *me* not to generalise. And Christian fundamentalism in America has everything to do with Israel,' answered Didier smoothly. 'Because in America it is not only extreme Zionist Jews who support Israeli militarism. It is also members of the Christian Far Right. And such Christians do not read the Bible *obliquely*, as a book full of nuance and mystery, but *literally*, as a timetable. They think history is over. They think Judgement Day is at hand.' He took a deep breath. 'Only in order for this Judgement Day to arrive, in order for the sheep to be separated from the goats, *the Jews must be back in Israel.* These particular Christians believe this is what the Bible is telling them. And that's why they support Israel. Not because they wish for Israel to prosper and be peaceful, but because they *want* the world to burn in fires; they *want* the Apocalypse.'

The solicitor was at this point sloppily drunk, drooping this way and that in his chair, and speaking in a kind of furry growl. 'Oh, come *on*, Didier. Those Christian fundamentalist madmen don't have that much power these days. It's the American Jews who are the problem. You'd think after the Holocaust they'd *want* to show *some* compassion. But not those filthy-rich American Jews and their Israeli parasites; oh no! They'd slaughter every last Palestinian man, woman and child, given half a chance.' He burped loudly. 'I mean, let's look at this thing objectively. Throughout history the Jews have always been troublemakers.' He took a slurp of wine. '*Jesus*, haven't we had enough of them? Between America and Israel they'll destroy the fucking world!'

Again Didier spoke quietly. 'Did you know that debates *do* go on in Israel itself, about the very nature of Zionism? Some Israelis do not confuse religion with nationalism. Some believe that Israel should be not a Jewish state but a secular one, in which all who wished to live there would have equal rights and liberties.' He paused to crush out his cigarette; Lily observed that his hand was trembling slightly. 'And I am sure you realise, Tom, that many of those on the Left in America, those Leftists who oppose American policy in the Middle East and who support Palestine, many of those are Jews.'

His eyes narrowed; for the first time that evening he looked angry. 'But perhaps you would decry the Jewish Left, as well? Perhaps you would call them mad anarchists, or Marxist agitators? Ah, yes; we all know the Jews on the Right are obscenely rich, while the Jews on the Left are filthy Commies who want to overthrow our capitalist system.' He gave a harsh laugh. 'Ah! We poor Jews. It seems we are to blame for everything.'

Lily thought about some of her relations. There had been a particular cousin of Jacob, a pale bespectacled man who had seemed to read all the time. His wife had recited nursery rhymes and given Lily squares of homemade honey cake to eat at the kitchen table. Such tender people, so different from Tom's image of Jews as twisted with rapacity or as territorial zealots.

Beside her, Jason said, 'Well, the Jews *are* competitive. We all know that. You've got to admire them, I guess. I mean, they do succeed and stuff. Look at how much money they make.'

Lily glared at him, this man who just a little while before had been trying, in an unabashedly competitive way, to insinuate himself into her professional world. Her voice shaking, she said to him, 'Do you truly know nothing of the ancient Jewish tradition of scholarship? Would you call those who study the kabbalah or debate the Talmud, who read all day long and care nothing for material things, would you call those people *competitive?*'

Jason laughed. 'Oh, those kinds of Jews are just *reacting* to the competitiveness. You know, all that mysticism and readings of the Torah and so forth, that's just a *reaction.*'

'Anyway,' said Doris primly, 'all I can say is that the intellectual Jew has a lot to answer for. The intellectual Jew cares about nothing but Israel.'

Lily hated that phrase, *the intellectual Jew*, with its echoes of Nazi bile about 'International Jewry'.

A man placed diagonally across from Lily laughed. He was German, had been born in Germany during the Second World War and had known great hardship as a child in its aftermath. Lily had spoken to him briefly before dinner and had found him a bit of a character, a handsome man with a perhaps exaggerated Teutonic accent. She'd gathered he had been an advertising copywriter. Now he said, 'Ach, vell, vat can von say? Ze Joos! Ze Joos are like vimmen! You can't live viz zem; you can't live vizout zem!' And he gave another laugh.

Lily's neighbour on her other side, a middle-aged painter of some renown, called Orla Smith, murmured, 'My dear man, was that an attempt to be *funny?* After all, not too long ago your lot would have been quite happy to live without them.'

Lily turned to look at her. She was tall, with a heavy intelligent face. Still in that low voice, she continued, 'You are disgusting. Doris and Jason and Tom, and you, also, Helmut. In this era, in the city of Leopold Bloom, in the presence of your distinguished host who happens to be Jewish. You are disgusting.'

The table fell silent as if stricken. Something about this Orla Smith, perhaps her quiet dignity, an air of moral authority, had made Jason squirm, Tom's mouth fall open, and Doris's blush deepen.

At the top of the table, Lucien said, 'Right. Let's call a halt. I think it's time you all went home. The party, I am afraid, is over. I do hope you at least enjoyed the food.'

In distress, Lily had been staring into her coffee cup. But now, glancing up at Didier, she saw, with a kind of horror, a kind of breaking of the heart, that his eyes were full of tears.

In the taxi back to Donnybrook she was silent until Nicholas gave her shoulder a consoling squeeze. Then she muttered, 'Oh, Lord, sometimes I hate myself.'

'You spoke up, Lily. You challenged them.'

She sighed, staring out at the lighted houses. 'I always assumed that in fairly civilised company, if a dinner guest said something racist or anti-Semitic, everyone else at the table would fall silent. They'd be *shocked*. And the racist guest would feel their disapproval and know he'd committed a breach of something important. But those stupid people tonight, they weren't at all embarrassed. They were *brazen*.'

Now it was Nicholas who sighed. 'A new form of anti-Semitism is on the rise, because of Israel's policies. And of course anti-Semites of the old school can seize on anti-Zionism these days as, you know, a cover-up for their obsession.'

Again Lily was silent before bursting out, 'I'm just so sick of myself. I'm a liar and a coward. I should have come clean. I should have let Didier know he wasn't the only Jew at that table.'

'We're all Jews, Lily, even an Ulster Protestant like me.' He gave a quiet laugh. 'You know that. When any one group is singled out for harm, we're all of us in danger.'

Next afternoon, while Nicholas was at the restaurant, Lily phoned Lucien and Didier. Lucien answered, which she'd expected since Didier spent most Saturdays at his antiques shop in Ranelagh.

'I thought I should speak to you,' she said. 'I wished to – I don't know – say something to make up for those horrible people.'

There was a short silence. Then Lucien said, 'Dear Lily, how kind, though *you* have nothing to apologise for. You didn't invite them, after all. We only asked Doris and Jason because they live next door, and Doris buys antiques. As for Tom, I didn't know he could be such an oaf. And I'll say nothing about Helmut. Anyway, you looked so sweet at the table with your *gamine* haircut.'

'Thank you. I had it done quite recently. Only the stylist told me my hair is getting *thin*.'

'Nonsense, your hair is lovely.' Another pause; then he said, 'Listen, it is such a beautiful day. Why don't we go for a walk in Stephen's Green?'

Waiting for Lucien, she looked at some small children feeding the ducks and for no reason felt tears behind her eyes. It was a splendid summer day, but she had suddenly realised she was the child of two mothers, a loving one and a viper, and she was plunged into confusion and guilt. When Lucien arrived he must have seen some of this in her face, for he took her hand without a word, and they began to walk along the paths.

She gazed with affection at his long head, and at his eyes that tapered upwards to the temples. His was an utterly Gallic face, she thought. Presently he asked what was wrong, and she said, 'May I ask you something very personal?'

They had settled on one of the benches. He lit a cigarette. 'Ask away.'

'When did you come out?'

'Of the closet, as they say in America?' He laughed. 'I find that expression quite funny, because of course the Americans mean a wardrobe, whereas I always picture some poor gay person huddled inside the toilet of a restaurant.' He seemed to hesitate. 'I don't know. It happened slowly. I fell in love, first with a teacher and then later on with another boy. Why do you ask?'

Avoiding the question, she persisted, 'But did you ever pretend to be straight? Was there a period in your life when you concealed the truth?'

'Oh, yes. I have had girlfriends. I have made love with women, which was pleasant though not exciting. As an adolescent I courted girls in order to pretend to the world and also to myself.' He examined his cigarette. 'But then I imagined living like that forever.'

'And you knew you couldn't?'

'I knew I couldn't.' He smiled. 'But why do you ask, Lily?'

Once more she evaded the question. 'Do you think they are also homophobic, some of your guests yesterday evening? I mean, they exposed their anti-Semitism because they didn't know about Didier. But what if they hadn't known you were a gay couple? Perhaps they would have been just as loathsome on that issue.'

'Possibly, although the Jewish thing is getting to be more and more of a problem, even on the Left. All kinds of seemingly open-minded people who'd never say a word against gays are bad-mouthing the Jews these days.'

She looked up at the trees. 'I'm partly Jewish too. I almost never speak about it.' She laughed. 'Well, I'm speaking about it now. But it's curious; I hadn't realised until just before you arrived how deeply ashamed I am. I'm ashamed of my mother who was slovenly and an alcoholic. I'm ashamed of where I come from, a very *middle* middle-class suburb in America.'

Lucien said, 'Why, Lily, I'd no idea you were from America.'

'Of course you had no idea. I've an English accent from my years at boarding school. And I've thrown a veil over my past, my truth, although I'm not entirely sure why . . . ' She pushed at the grass with the toe of her shoe. 'Maybe I have concealed my Jewishness as well as my American origins because of this longing I've always had to be a European. And Europe is a Christian conti-nent.' Saying this, she saw in her mind's eye a myriad of churches: Norman towers; Gothic spires; chancels and naves and rose win-dows. 'Europe is a Christian continent,' she repeated.

They were silent a moment. Then Lucien said, 'Didier once told me a story. His people were originally from Russia. And he had this wonderful Russian grandmother. As you can imagine, she went through terrible times. As a little child she barely survived the Holocaust, and of course many of her family perished. Yet Didier says she was never bitter, and that in fact she was one of those perfect grannies, you know, like something out of a storybook, always baking cakes and giving presents.'

Lily smiled, thinking she'd have liked a granny. But the temperamental and disconcertingly lithe Jacob was the only grandparent she could remember.

Lucien continued, 'Yet Didier told me that even though he loved this grandmother, he was still ashamed of her when he was small. He was ashamed of her thick accent and her old-fashioned ways. He thought the other children would laugh at her. Perhaps they did laugh at her.' He halted to crush out his cigarette. 'But as Didier got a bit older and less concerned about what others might think, he realised how wonderful she was, what a wonderful woman, so learned, so well-read. She spoke Russian, French, German and Yiddish; she'd read poetry, fiction, history and philosophy in all those languages. She was a brilliant piano player and discussed political theory, science and the visual arts. All in her thick accent, in her plain style, wearing her frumpy clothes, her hands gnarled from hardship.'

'She was a true European,' Lily murmured.

Lucien laughed. 'People go on about how materialistic the Jews are. But the Jews I knew in France aspired always to carry their riches in the head. All of that learning, it was so precious. If some official told these friends of mine that they were not permitted to own land, if their goods were taken from them, still no one could touch those riches in their mind.'

He made a very French gesture involving his hands, shoulders and mouth. 'You know, Lily, I *can* understand why you conceal your Jewish side. It could be part of your ancestral memory. Telling the truth gets one into trouble, so it is better to lie.' He paused. 'And Nicholas is a bit like you, afraid to trust the world, yes?'

She gave him a startled look. 'How did you know?'

Lucien said, 'I don't *know*. It's only something I am feeling. He seems . . . cautious, at times, disquieted. And he has no Northern accent, as you have no American one.'

She thought of the things she loved in Nicholas: his sense of humour, the downward curve of his mouth when he smiled, his body and hands, his cooking. And that nameless thing which is the axis of love. Then once more she considered how ashamed of herself she was, a little child with albino hair and terrified eyes forever crouched in a corner, old scapegoat, old liar that she was. Lucien was right: both she and Nicholas were afraid to trust the world. But surely they were learning to trust each other?

Chapter VIII

Hannah's Wine Bar
Dublin 2
by Lily Murphy

Hannah's specialises in French wines and cheeses, which compels me to recall one of my favourite stories about wine. In France, recently, an oenophile came upon a wine cellar that had lain abandoned for centuries. Entering it gingerly, as though afraid to awaken the slumbering bottles, he marvelled at them, gleaming dully through their films of cobweb and dust. He extracted one sixteenth-century bottle, which he and his friends proceeded to open, each taking a hasty swallow. And for that one evanescent moment, just before the wine soured to vinegar, the flavour of Rabelais's time was on their tongue.

The reason I love this story is that it illustrates how wine is a living thing, always mysteriously growing, changing. And good cheese is the same, though generally it must be made from raw milk. I lament the strict EU regulations that forbid the importing of unpasteurised cheeses. A raw milk brie, for instance, its rind mottling like rust as it ages, its interior beginning to flow, is so luscious compared to a brie made from pasteurised milk, which will refuse to ripen, maintaining a rubbery texture until it simply goes off.

I hope I am not being indiscreet by revealing that Hannah's Wine Bar offers an abundance of beautiful raw milk cheeses from France and Italy. Perhaps these are contra-band, smuggled into Ireland past the insensitive noses of customs officials, but I believe there is a dispensation for cer-tain raw milk cheeses which have matured awhile, thus elim-inating the possibility of dangerous microbes, or whatever it is that people fear. Anyway, Hannah's has all kinds of fine goat's cheeses, some that are fresh and fluffy, with the bland flavour of new milk, others encrusted with ash or herbs, still others that are well-aged and sturdy. The lunchtime plate of French and Irish goat's cheeses, accompanied by a green salad and a glass of Côtes du Rhône, is a splendid value.

At lunch only cold dishes appear on the menu, but that is no hardship, since they are so varied, and go so well with wine. One of the more pleasant plates is – and please do not laugh – egg mayonnaise! You may associate egg mayo-nnaise with indifferent country hotel cooking, or bad wedding breakfasts. You may picture overcooked eggs, with black-encircled yolks, placed unceremoniously on some tired lettuce and drenched in salad cream. But a properly executed oeuf mayonnaise is like a celestial picnic. First you must have an utterly fresh, free-range egg, and to cook it properly you should never actually boil it. Plunging a delicate egg into roiling water only creates a tough white, and a dry yolk surrounded by that unpleasant green-black line. On the other hand, simmering an egg gently for the right length of time produces a tender white and a yolk that is luscious, brightly coloured and still slightly moist at the centre. Then of course there is the matter of the mayonnaise. At Hannah's it is, of course, homemade (despite EU edicts about raw eggs), its richness leavened by mustard and lemon. It is served as a pretty swirl on top of the halved egg, and the garnish of crudités (carrottes rapee, céleri rémoulade, black olives and an artichoke heart) is delicious as well, especially with the restaurant's homemade French bread.

Another humble yet extraordinary dish here is the cold lamb with salad. I have always been puzzled as to why more people do not serve lamb cold. It is gorgeous in a sandwich, just as nice as cold beef or chicken, yet it is seldom offered either in restaurants or people's homes. Hannah's cold lamb is savoury and tender, liberally seasoned with garlic and rosemary. A little pot of that splendid mayonnaise accompanies it, along with an excellent green salad.

Of course I should speak about the wines. Mostly French, they are uniformly good and moderately priced, with a special bottle featured each month. There are some fine Loire Valley wines, including a Chinon (Rabelais's favourite tipple), as well as a fragrant Touraine. And the

167

variety of Beaujolais, from aromatic Morgon through the heavier Chiroubles, to glorious Saint-Amour, is marvellous. There is an array of white Burgundies, and also a fine, light Frascati. Hannah's offers no 'new world' wines, so as to concentrate properly on the vineyards of France and Italy, which seems sensible, and certainly results in some discerning selections that are not at all expensive.

Two or three cooked plates are on the dinner menu, all simple and good: grilled salmon or plaice, minute steak with green pepper sauce, lamb chops or roast chicken. Hannah, a young woman with a serene smile and long hair pale as the flesh of lemons, told me she herself has no palate for sweets; therefore very few are on offer. You can take apple tart or ice cream, but I would recommend the cheese; or, if you must have a sweet course, then the fresh berries served with a glass of Sauternes is lovely.

Hannah's is a large room with pink tablecloths, and a friendly staff. They play mostly jazz, very good stuff, and late each Friday night the tables are pushed to the side for dancing, which goes on until about three in the morning.

★

The last time Lily saw her parents was not in London but Paris, where the magazine had sent her on a six month assignment in 1998. She was staying there with her old school friend Vivian, a Francophile since their journey to Nice, and now a painter like her father. She was living in an atelier in the fourteenth arrondissement, across the street from a primary school, so that the high-pitched voices of children, like starlings, would weave in and out of her window while she tried to paint the rich silver light of her adopted city.

Lily brought Vivian to the restaurants with her, and every evening, before dinner, they took an aperitif standing at the counter of Le Lyonnais, Vivian's favourite local café. One night while they drank there, Vivian suddenly asked, 'Do you remember milk bottles? Did you have milk bottles in New York, pint bottled delivered by a real milkman?'

'Yes, when I was very little. Only they were quart bottles. I suppose everything had to be *bigger* in America. Squat quart bottles, with ruffled paper tops, delivered by a milkman dressed all in white like a bottle of milk himself. Pasteurised. Homogenised.'

'Not in England. I mean *not* homogenised. There was a layer of cream at the top. And the pint bottles were slender, with long necks.'

Lily suddenly remembered a particular Vermeer, of a girl standing at a window with the sunlight shining through her wimple. And also the Irishman William Leach, his painting of Breton girls walking in a green-gold wood, their white veils glowing. That light, like milk clouding against the sides of a glass bottle. She smiled to herself, thinking that under Vivian's influence she was beginning to see things in a painterly way.

'Ah, Vivian,' she said. 'We remember milk bottles! We're growing old.'

'Speak for yourself,' Vivian replied in her blunt style. An admirer of the American vernacular, she was forever trying to cultivate a kind of New York argot, though she often got it wrong. Now they began to argue over the matter in a friendly way, with

Lily deploring the jargon of commerce so many Americans seemed to use: 'I hate those harsh expressions like "What's the deal?" or "I don't buy that" or "Here's the bottom line".'

Vivian replied that the American idiom was salted with an exciting vigour, a pleasing toughness. 'Anyway,' she continued, 'Why do you keep referring to Americans as "they"? As if you weren't from there yourself.'

Just at that moment, an elderly American couple walked up beside them. And how was Lily immediately sure they were American? She supposed it was their clothes. The man was wearing one of those exercise suits made of some brightly coloured synthetic fabric the name of which she did not know, but which was light and shiny as foil; the woman sported a pink jacket and white sun visor, as if she were intending to play golf. Lily thought she looked hard, the woman, that there was something overly controlled even in the furls of her grey hair, while the man's smile was all too guileless. Yet even as she thought these things she knew they were unfair. She *knew* Paris was full of intelligent and interesting Americans. She considered Edith Wharton inviting Henry James to tea at her house in the Faubourg Saint-Germain. But she couldn't overcome her intolerance.

She looked once more at the couple, standing uneasily in their sherbet-coloured clothes before the *zinc*, while all about them the waiters moved swiftly, the *habitués* called greetings to one another, young couples smoked and touched each other's hands, and an old woman with masses of white hair read *Le Monde*. All the bustle and intimacy of French café life, which had daunted Lily, too, when she'd first come with Vivian so many years before. People had been charitable to them then, perhaps because the young are generally forgiven their gaucherie. But the American pair beside her were not young, though they looked vulnerable. Lily thought, *What right have I to judge them?* Vivian must have been surveying them as well, for now she said, 'Lily, when was the last time you saw your mum and dad?'

'A couple of years ago,' she mumbled. She paused. 'As a matter of fact, my mother wrote me a few weeks before I left to come here. She said they were considering a journey to England. Only now I'm in France, so I don't know . . . '

'Tell them to come to France, why don't you? It's a kind of neutral territory, isn't it? See them in France, which is neither their home nor yours. It would be easier than either London or New York, don't you think?'

Lily gave a sigh, fiddling with her wineglass. And yet again she glanced at the American couple. They had ordered glasses of beer, in English. But Vivian was right: why did she insist on referring to Americans as *them* and *they*? When ordinary things, a smell of steam heat in an apartment, or the dry metallic light after a fall of snow, would spirit her back straightaway to her first life in New York, a city she loved despite herself.

The couple looked at her, and the woman, whom she had earlier dismissed as hard, suddenly smiled, a smile of such warmth and open-heartedness that, absurdly, Lily felt a prickle of tears behind her eyes.

Her father said, 'So we were in this restaurant in . . . Brittany, was it? Little place. And the waiter brought over the menu and it was *just in French.'* He paused, eyes wide for effect. 'No translation into English. It was as if they'd never seen Americans before.'

Lily tried to speak evenly. 'Well, Dad. You were in a French restaurant. In France.' But he shook his head, still astonished by the memory of that benighted place. She realised she should drop the subject, but her own indignation forced her to go on, 'And don't you think it was a good sign, that they weren't cosseting the tourists with special menus in English? The food was probably lovely.'

He glanced at Caroline, as if to say, *There goes Lily, being difficult again.* But she persisted, 'And anyway, what *do* you mean about them never seeing *Americans* before, because they had no menu in English? Do you really think only Americans speak English, Dad? What about the Canadians and the Australians and the Irish? To say nothing of the English themselves, who only happened to *invent* the language?'

She was dismayed to have brought them to a restaurant she was reviewing. They were flustering her so badly, she could barely register her surroundings. And it was a charming place, not far from Vivian's studio, fairly *raffiné* though unpretentious, with a menu of the day composed of things bought that morning from the local market. But she was beginning to feel marooned from the relaxed-looking people encircling them. Her mother stared at a woman who had just come in with her little dog on a lead. 'It's the custom here,' Lily tried to explain. 'People are allowed to bring their dogs into the cafés and restaurants.'

Her mother frowned, and drank some water, while her father glanced worriedly at his wife, anxious, as always, to appease her; sensitive, as always, to any stiffness in her posture, her slightest frown, as he had never been sensitive to Lily's distress. In fact the two of them wore an anxious, defeated look. They seemed to huddle in their corner, her greying powerless father and her mother who could no longer drink and who had grown old, but whose humours her father continued to serve. In that way, at least, he was still reliable. It occurred to Lily that they were both afraid of life and perhaps had always been so. Now her father pressed on peevishly, 'And did I tell you, when we first arrived in London and we were taking the bus to the National Gallery— '

'We had shopping bags,' said her mother.

'We got into the bus with our shopping bags, and the seat beside us was empty so we put the bags there. But then the driver says, "That's not allowed. No bags on the seats." The English are so rigid! He probably thought we looked like Americans. Well, we *are* Americans, aren't we, Caroline? So what! Why did a bus driver have to teach us a lesson? Anyway, we put the bags on the floor, where they fell over whenever the bus turned a corner. It was a *nightmare.*'

'Hardly a nightmare,' Lily murmured, thinking that their talent for histrionics was clearly undiminished. And she couldn't credit their story, because on every London bus the driver was cordoned off from the passengers and only the conductor spoke to them. 'How was the Calais ferry?' she asked, dreading the reply.

They had been served country bread and a bowl of olives, and now the waiter brought the starters. Her parents had left the ordering to Lily who had chosen, for her mother, a dish of courgette flowers stuffed with a mousse of crab. It looked delicious, all green and coral, but Caroline pushed at it with her fork and said, 'This sauce is too rich. You *know* I have to watch my cholesterol, Lily.'

Her father stared glumly at his Provençal fish soup and muttered, 'It smells like fish.'

She suppressed laughter, but was also feeling guilty. She *should* have remembered her mother's cholesterol. And she knew she was probably being too harsh. Obviously her parents were truculent because they felt hurt, and rightly so, by a daughter who had made her life far from where they considered home, and was clearly reluctant to meet them. She also knew that her embarrassment at being in their presence was juvenile, the attitude of an adolescent who has been dragged to a restaurant by her totally uncool parents. But she had left them when she was, indeed, an adolescent.

Her mother answered, 'The Channel crossing was alright, until we went into the wrong tea room.'

'The wrong tea room?' Once more Lily was caught between embarrassment and an almost desperate desire to laugh.

She explained, 'There's a tea room for first class passengers on the Dover to Calais ferry. Apparently – we learned this later – people save their money for a whole year to buy the right clothes to wear for tea in this first class salon. But your father and I didn't know, and we just wanted tea. So we opened the door of this first class tea room, and we were, you know, wearing our ordinary clothes— '

'We probably looked like Americans,' repeated her father.

'And everybody stared at us. The women were all wearing those ridiculous English hats, and flowery dresses. You know, like the Queen. Can you imagine saving up for a year to buy clothes like that? So the whole room froze, with everybody scowling at us. It was terrible.'

Lily thought, in yet another moment of grim hilarity, that perhaps her parents had been on drugs during their crossing. Perhaps someone had surreptitiously given them a hash brownie or a fragment of acid, after which they'd had an hallucination in common, where they are gazing upon a genteel, nautical tea room *that does not exist*. A kind of Lewis Carroll for grownups.

She was grateful when the main courses arrived, since at least they were a distraction. And it seemed this time she'd made the right choices, keeping to seafood, and ordering simple things: sole meunière for her father, sea bass for her mother, and John Dory for herself. Squeezing lemon over their fish, her parents looked pleased, and things did get better; the atmosphere grew lighter.

In fact her mother queried her in a way that seemed genuine. She had been examining her fish knife, and now she asked, 'Lily, how do you feel about the more formal way of life here in Europe?' She smiled almost sardonically. 'Of course your grandfather *adores* it, misses it in New York. I used to say, "But Papa, Europe became a charnel house for your people! How can you cherish it after that?" And he would answer, "I just can't help it. I have never lost the *dream* of Europe." It's partly the ballet, I guess. Every dancer seems to worship France and Russia. Though I think it's also his temperament.'

Lily hesitated, because she was remembering the free-for-all at the dinner table when she was growing up, and how she had come to feel infected by her mother's slatternly ways, as if she, Lily, were not contained within herself, but had become like some fluid slopping over the sides of a cup. All over the place. *Like her mother.*

And now she wondered, was this why she had grown up to be something of a fuddy-duddy, preferring old-fashioned decorum to spontaneity? Once more she glanced round at the other tables, at the mainly middle-aged people eating their stylish meals. It was an appealing scene, but perhaps also a bit boring for a girl in her twenties? Only it was so soothing, after those disorderly early years. Finally the substance was contained within the cup, and such an ambrosial one, with its patina of history.

Carefully, she ventured, 'I admire America for how it has over-come certain stuffy Old World notions. But I suppose every society tries to reconcile basic needs – like eating – with the yearnings of the spirit. And I love how the Europeans have managed it, how they have sweetened our needs, our instincts, with ceremony.' She refrained from saying, 'Mother. Caroline. It's not really that I pre-fer Europe to America, per se. It's that I prefer Europe to *you*. I prefer Old World *politesse* to your drunken abuse of me – is that so hard to understand?'

Her mother muttered, 'Well, lots of Americans become expa-triates for a while, but eventually almost all of them go back.'

Lily wished to say she was pleased to have passed through the mirror – like Alice – and to have made Europe her home. But regarding Caroline's hurt face, she said nothing. Her mother went on, 'Your grandfather always wanted to make you into a European – I guess he succeeded.' She gave an acerbic smile. 'But there are things you don't know about him. You think he's romantic, but there are things I never told you.'

Curiously, Lily was not surprised. She had always known, in some place inside herself older even than words, that there was a secret connected to her grandfather, and that this secret lay like a shadow over her parents' life and therefore over her own. She waited for her mother to continue.

Only then her father cried in his terrible whingeing voice, 'Caroline, come *on*. Why are you talking about that *now*. Don't upset yourself. It's *late*.'

Her mother sighed. 'Yes, it's late. We'd better get back to the hotel.'

'Please,' Lily said softly, refusing to look at her craven father, with whom she was furious. 'Please tell me.'

But Caroline shook her head, 'Not now.'

There was one final disappointment. As they were preparing to leave, her mother said forthrightly, 'It *is* good to see you.' She seemed to hesitate. 'I am sorry, Lily, that you have grown so separate from us. I'm sorry we disappointed you.'

Lily had been gathering up her scarf and handbag but now she stopped, arrested by her mother's candour. It was, she hoped (and also feared) an important moment. 'How was it – how do you think – you disappointed me?'

Caroline laughed. 'Sometimes I think about how you had hay fever. How you would stay in the house on a bright summer day, because of the pollen. As if the air itself had become a menace. And I think I should have breast fed you, in spite of my doctor who preferred formula for babies. Breast milk is supposed to contain antibodies, you know, to prevent allergies. I should have nursed you, despite my doctor.'

Lily was trembling. 'Is there anything else? Do you think . . . you were sometimes excessively angry?'

'Oh, come on,' intervened her father again. 'Lily, please don't upset your mother.'

This time Lily glared at him, observing that whenever she was with her parents she felt oppressed – so oppressed! Once more she remembered Lewis Carroll: an enlarged Alice having to squeeze her limbs into a room that had become frighteningly miniscule.

Her mother gave another laugh. 'Yes, sometimes. I shouted too much. My voice is very strong. I always got the lead in school plays when I was a kid, because of this robust voice of mine. So when I shouted at you it must have seemed like quite a roar, and your little face would go white with fear. I must have sounded more furious than I really was. I *am* sorry about that. But of course mothers do get angry. It's natural. I would shout at you when you didn't clean your room or finish your homework. That's just natural, isn't it?'

So she would always pretend none of it had happened. She would insist they were a family from some 1950s film or television series, Dad, Mom, little Lily and Woof-Woof, though they'd never had a dog. Or even a goldfish. 'Yes,' Lily murmured, 'Just natural.'

Though what she was picturing was an early memory, one of the few not lost in the general blur, of her gin-soaked mother dragging her across the kitchen floor by her hair. Yes, by the hair.

After her parents had returned to New York, Lily and Vivian were relaxing on Vivian's studio floor one evening, eating chunks of Gruyère and drinking red wine. Lying on her back with a hand behind her head, Vivian observed, 'All in all, Lily, you are not a woman-to-woman kind of woman. Are you?'

'Am I not?' She took a gulp of wine. She was feeling at once wistful and festive after her parents' departure. And since Vivian had just sold a painting they'd decided to get tipsy that night and at this point were well on the way. 'No, I suppose I'm not.'

Vivian hoisted herself up on an elbow. 'What I mean is, you don't have lots of women friends, do you? I'm nearly your only one.

You give the impression of being often alone and . . . cautious.'

Lily considered Hugo, with whom she'd recently broken up. She answered slowly, 'I *am* a bit afraid of women.' She amended quickly, 'Not you, Vivian. I mainly fear a certain unconscious kind of woman, who would tempt a man away from me, but not even alertly, like a proper coquette. It's an all-over-the-place, *slumberous* kind of seductress that frightens me. I don't know. I'm not putting this very well.'

'That's okay,' said Vivian, turning onto her back again, 'Let's have another drink.'

Lily poured more wine, and thought about the women she liked: Vivian, of course, and her lovely mother. And she did have warm relations with female colleagues – even her slightly intimidating editor – though it was true she was probably not a 'woman-to-woman' woman.

'Anyhow, it's not *fair*,' Vivian grumbled. 'It's not *fair* that *you* should feel insecure about other women. After all, you're beautiful and I'm just ordinary-looking. It's *me* who has the right to be insecure, Lily.'

'I don't feel beautiful,' answered Lily honestly. 'And you are *not* ordinary-looking, with your blue-black hair. Besides, have you ever noticed, in novels, how the more interesting characters are often plain, like Jane Eyre?'

Vivian threw her a quizzical look and, instead of answering, said, 'You know, you should have introduced me to your mum and dad. I'd have liked to meet them. It's as if – I don't know – it's as if you don't quite trust me.'

'Oh, Vivian, it's them I don't trust.' Lily regarded her friend who was still lying on her back with her hair spread out around her.

And she gave a silent sigh, wishing she had nice presentable parents, like Vivian's, instead of her own, of whom she was so ashamed.

★

Nicholas. Why did she love him so? What was it about him, this man with his sombre Northern past? He told her that for him it was the same. He'd had lovers before with whom he should have had a closer rapport, since they were from the North of Ireland too. Yet only with each other had Lily and Nicholas begun to touch a certain source. They had described around themselves a circle, within which they were both, finally, beginning to feel at home. *But why you?* each would think, touching hands in bed or across a table. *Why should it be you, and not someone else?*

Whatever the reason, she was starting to know him inside herself. She *felt* the rain-swept street where he had grown up, that house full of Royal Family memorabilia, the oilcloth-covered table with its bottles of ketchup and HP sauce, at which he had done his school exercises and dreamt of escape.

One morning, on his day off, they went to the National Gallery.

Nicholas brought her to see Caravaggio's *The Taking of Christ*. Some force in it impressed her: the shadows, the burnished light, the urgency of the soldiers and the anguish of the disciples, with, off to the left and somehow alone amid the confusion, the sorrowful face of Jesus, suffering Judas to kiss him.

Nicholas explained how Baroque art nearly always suggests agitation, life captured *in media res*, hence the surging cloaks, and the subjects positioned off-centre and *pushed* by the artist into the foreground. He said he thought this painting was gorgeous for the soldier's metal-sheathed arm, extended to grasp its quarry; and also for the hand of Judas, clutching at Christ in an imploring, intimate, shocking way.

'I didn't realise,' she said, 'that you knew so much about painting.'

He smiled almost shyly.

They had a light lunch at an Italian shop that sold cheeses, salamis, olives and wine, and that doubled as a café. Then as they were strolling down Dame Street, Nicholas suggested they see a film at the Irish Film Institute, which was showing a retrospective of boxing movies.

Lily said, 'I *know* there are some really great films about boxing. But I don't like them. I don't like those scenes of sweaty gyms, and smoky boxing rings, and men with bashed-up faces, and managers who call the hero "Champ".'

'But they're showing *Gentleman Jim* today. With Errol Flynn before he got dissipated.'

'Weren't Errol Flynn's politics very bad?'

'Appalling. His family were from Belfast, though. Actually there are loads of famous boxers from Belfast. Like Rinty Monaghan. Never heard of him? He used to celebrate his victories by singing *Danny Boy* in the ring. And of course there's little Wayne McCullough, the Pocket Rocket. Come to think of it, most of the great Belfast boxers have been rather small. Perhaps it's their diet.'

Lily stopped in the road. 'You continue to amaze me. In the morning I learn you know all about Baroque painting, and now I discover you're an expert on boxing.'

He gave another shy smile. 'Well, boxing was important in my part of Belfast. And Ireland really has produced some fantastic fighters. But you know something? Many Irish boxers were reluctant to go to the States – despite the lure of big bucks – because the Americans would do dastardly things like make them fight in Las Vegas, in the sweltering climate.'

This time it was he who halted. 'Only one time the Irish got their revenge by doing more or less the same thing. A South American came to Belfast to fight Barry McGuigan, the Clones Cyclone. But they billeted this South American in your typical Belfast B&B. And he couldn't stand the food.'

'He was like you!'

'Yes, like me. He couldn't stand all those Ulster fries, morning after morning. And the cod and chips for dinner. So he stopped eating. And on the day of the fight he was too weak to box properly. I think he might even have fainted.'

A light rain had started; they continued walking, hand in hand. Nicholas said, 'Would you like to hear another boxing-and-food story from Belfast? There was this good Northern fighter who was finally beaten by a Mexican. So he became *obsessed* by Mexican food. In fact, he opened a Mexican restaurant close to the Ulster Museum, with a Mexican chef and subtle Mexican dishes; not that Tex-Mex rubbish but the real thing: chipotle sauce and ceviche and so on, right in the heart of provincial wee Belfast.'

'All right,' conceded Lily. 'I admit you make boxing sound interesting. I suppose we can see the Errol Flynn.'

She actually found *Gentleman Jim* interesting enough, with the young Flynn's swashbuckling style; anyway she loved the cinema. Though she seldom had a chance to go, since reviewing restaurants seemed to take up an extraordinary amount of time, all those dishes to sample and then the articles to write and file. It sounded such a plum of a job (so to speak) when she described it to others, but it could be tedious and painstaking or even nightmarish, depending on the restaurant. Anyway, today was a day off for her as well, and she found herself feeling happy and peaceful.

After the movie they walked along Grafton Street in the soft rain. Somehow it had got late and they were hungry. They turned down a quiet passage and descended into an underground wine bar that Nicholas loved, but where Lily had never been.

Its lighting was low. There was a long bar, and a long mirror in which the whole of the small restaurant – a few banquettes and tables for two or four – was reflected. The place struck her as very French, with its candles and red napkins, and Edith Piaf's voice in the background. On the other hand it did not evoke Paris so much as some southern place: an Arabian carpet decorated one wall, and there were filigreed lamps on the counter. Then Nicholas introduced her to the chef, a Tunisian man with vast eyes, and she realised why she'd had that immediate impression of North Africa, or perhaps a Mediterranean port like Nice or Marseilles, rather than Paris.

The chef insisted on making a special meal for them. They were both content, Nicholas because he did not have to cook and Lily because she did not have to eat professionally. They were served a first course of scallops in a cream sauce scented with pastis, along with a half bottle of Muscadet.

The main course was shank of lamb seasoned with cumin. And the waitress opened a bottle of Chiroubles, which was dark as blackberries, with a rich aroma. They ate in silence for a while, intent on the soft succulent meat; then Nicholas caressed her hand across the table and said warmly, 'Your wrist is so small.'

Lily smiled. 'You know, something I have never written about, although I write about food the whole time, is how obsessed people are with dieting, especially women. It's hard to believe that women used not to diet. They just ate. They ate for the joy of it. And their beauty was various. Some women were voluptuous and others thin, but they were all considered nice-looking.'

'I hate it in the restaurant when a woman, usually a young woman, comes in and asks for sickroom dishes like plain poached fish or pasta with nothing on top.'

She sighed. 'It's weird, isn't it? We have such abundance that we're afraid of getting fat, and so we dine on plain pasta. On the other hand there's still so much famine in the world. I haven't written about that either, the *politics* of food, how these big conglomerates control the industry. How they pour grain into the sea while babies die of hunger. How they blanch flour until all its nutrients are scrubbed away so that it will last longer and make them a larger profit. How they hydrogenate fats, which renders them more stable but chemically rancid. How they've convinced mothers to buy expensive, nutritionally empty formula for their babies. Obviously that's why a restaurant called 'Hungry Grass' made me so furious. Did you know there used to be ten thousand varieties of rice in Asia, and now there are only one thousand? For marketing reasons.'

Nicholas said, 'Lily, why *don't* you write about those things? Why don't you write a book, a proper book? You don't want to do restaurant columns forever. It's about time you wrote a book.'

She laughed. 'I could try, but only if *you* wrote a book. You should write a cookery book. And there should be a picture of you on the cover, smiling, with a knife and an onion positioned artistically on the counter before you. It would be an instant best seller.'

The waitress asked if they would like dessert, but they decided to linger over the wine instead and then have coffee. Lily said, 'Tell me a story about when you were a boy, in Belfast.'

He was silent, looking downwards. She was suddenly conscious that they were the only customers, and that the candles burning on the empty tables made the room look a bit like a chapel. Then he muttered, 'I don't know. It was pretty rough, where I grew up, as I've told you. I don't know . . . ' He glanced up with a thin smile. 'I'd prefer not to go there just now. You know I've something to tell you, but not now.'

'I understand,' she answered smoothly, as she had done once before, though she was feeling baffled, as on that night in his kitchen when he had nearly vouchsafed her what was probably his deepest confidence, and also, further in the past, at that Parisian restaurant when her mother had alluded to a secret before falling suddenly, stubbornly silent.

In the next few weeks, Lily looked back on their day off wistfully, because they were both suddenly very busy. Aer Lingus's in-flight magazine had given the Matisse a big write-up, which meant that a new surge of transatlantic and European tourists, in addition to the usual local gourmets, was flooding into it nearly every evening. And not only had Dublin seemed to blossom overnight with new restaurants, two established places had just been awarded Michelin stars, which merited more visits to each. So Lily had the impression she was barely seeing Nicholas. At breakfast he would mutter things like, 'That new chef at the Auberge Saint Antoine is doing a terrine of suckling pig with hazelnuts. I'll make one with pistachios; much better,' before hurrying out the door. And at bedtime they were both sometimes too tired for even a goodnight kiss.

In the midst of all this, Lily woke up one morning feeling decidedly queasy, or 'green', as the girls at school used to say. She rolled over onto her stomach, groaning. A bout of gastritis was a disaster in her line of work. She'd eaten oysters the night before; they'd had the quicksilver flavour of exquisite freshness, but perhaps one of them had been a bit off, after all?

When Nicholas came out from the shower, towelling his hair, she said, 'Is there a patron saint of stomachs?'

Of course the Protestant Nicholas laughed. 'You could say a prayer to that guy who's in charge of lost causes, or is it hopeless cases?'

She groaned again. 'I'm not being facetious; I really would like to pray to someone. I think I've got food poisoning.'

In the course of the morning, while drinking tea, she did utter a kind of wordless prayer, which might have worked, for by lunchtime she was feeling much better. But two days later she was settling down to an afternoon meal at a new 'international bistro' – whatever that meant – when she felt ill in a different way.

It was simply the asparagus, an attractive starter of green asparagus glossed with hollandaise sauce. Normally she loved asparagus, but now even its vernal, grass-like smell filled her mouth with a fluid of nausea. She smoothed the napkin over her knees, raised one stalk to her lips and managed to eat it. But that smell! And the thick butter-flavour of the hollandaise! She stared helplessly at the plate until a waiter came over to ask what was wrong.

She smiled weakly. 'Sorry. It's lovely. I'm just – I'm not feeling very well. Sorry.'

She was thinking she'd have to abandon the meal altogether, which would not please her editor. But when the main course (osso buco) arrived, she found she could eat it not only dutifully but with relish.

Later that same afternoon, Sylvie rang. 'I'm feeling very odd these days,' Lily told her. 'Tired, and a bit off my food, which is not a good idea in my profession.'

'Perhaps you need a tonic,' Sylvie suggested. Then she lowered her voice and continued excitedly, 'Lily, I've the most exciting news. I wanted to tell you first, before anyone else. Perhaps you didn't know, darling, perhaps I haven't told you because – well – it *is* rather private, but Will and I were trying for *ages* to make a baby. And this morning I learnt we've finally done it. I'm positively *pregnant.*'

Lily gazed out of Nicholas's kitchen window, at the rainy street where a little boy of eleven or so, wearing red trousers and carrying a red umbrella, was walking his floppy-eared spaniel.

All her life she had lived as the child of her mother; she had never once considered how to live as the mother of a child. It sometimes seemed that everyone – or at least Caroline and Nicholas – was keeping secrets from her. Yet she realised now that for several weeks she had been keeping an immense secret from herself.

Part Two

Chapter IX

Lily was more or less living with Nicholas, but her magazine had paid the Arts Club in advance, so she kept her room there, visiting it sometimes to work or read, or to collect post that the Club had neglected to forward. The day after her chat with Sylvie, she was there when her mobile rang.

It was her father. The moment she heard his timid-sounding voice, she knew something was wrong. 'Is anyone ill?' she asked sharply. 'Is it Jacob, Dad?'

'No. He's fine.' She sensed an asperity, as if he half believed her grandfather remained healthy through sheer obduracy. 'No, Lily. It's your mother. She's very ill. I'm afraid you had better come over here, if you – if you want to see her before . . . '

Lily felt the nothing feeling of shock. She questioned him automatically, and learnt that it was her mother's liver, as she had bitterly suspected, and that there was very little time, perhaps as little as a week, since she was beginning to experience 'multiple organ failure'. Then she was kept busy with phone calls to Aer Lingus and to her editor in London. When she rang Nicholas he sounded distracted, and she could hear raised voices and the clanging of metal behind him; the lunch crowd were just beginning to pour in.

'I know you haven't much time,' she said hurriedly. 'But I needed to hear your voice.' She told him the news. 'The airline was remarkably helpful. They actually have something called "compassion flights". They got me onto tomorrow's plane. A return; I'm coming back in a fortnight.'

Her voice trembled then and she remembered Lucien referring to her 'ancestral memory'. It was true; she was afraid to leave Dublin and Nicholas. She feared – what, exactly? A Customs official fastening a baleful eye on her and demanding that she tell him why she had chosen to *live abroad* and not *in her own country*; a Passport Control man announcing something was amiss and they'd have to detain her in America: that ancestral memory of a sharp knock on the door and then one's mother or father being taken away; a subsequent fear of officialdom, of men in uniform. She was afraid to go; she feared she would be punished for her happiness in Dublin by being forbidden to return to it.

And how did she feel about her mother dying? Bitterness, and love, dragging itself up from her depths despite herself: bitterness – and love.

That night, the pair of them upset for her, she and Nicholas drank too much, a bottle of Saumur he'd brought back from the restaurant, followed by quite a few draughts of Calvados. And next day, on the plane, drinking litres of water while refusing the pallid meal, Lily was not oblivious to the irony of flying to New York with a hangover, to see, probably for the last time, the mother whose drinking had blighted her early life.

At Kennedy Airport she was struck by the flat, murky quality of the light, and by the heat. It recalled her immediately to her far-away past, to summers smelling of fuel, burnt tarmac and arid grass, to hot nights followed by a dawn like bronze and then more heat all day long, to the bruised sky before a thunderstorm, and then the evanescent freshness of summer air after rain. Befuddled as any tourist, she clambered into a taxi and directed it to the Manhattan hospital where her mother lay dying.

The driver said, 'Humid enough for you?'

He looked like one of those old-fashioned New York taxi drivers one saw in films, sturdy and grizzled, and obviously eager to talk with his passenger.

'It's dreadful,' she agreed.

'Yeah. Especially when you're not used to it. You're from England, right?'

'Yes,' she sighed.

'I like the accent. Listen, just relax and enjoy the air conditioning. I always keep the car air conditioned this time of year. If you get out of my taxi all hot and sweaty, what's the point, know what I mean? Over there across the river is the Empire State Building, if you've never been to New York before.'

'I have been here before,' she murmured, gazing across the East River at the pinnacles of Manhattan. 'Once before.'

The blend of familiarity and strangeness was giving her an eerie feeling of dislocation. Her mind and heart were still in Dublin, but her weary body was in a yellow taxi plunging through Manhattan in the middle of a hot afternoon. The sky here was a hard blanched blue, cloudless, and the street corners thronged with irritable-looking people. She recoiled from the city, freighted as it was with sad memories, and yet, reluctantly, something in her warmed, also. She was remembering, she was remembering.

There was Park Avenue with its parade of flowers down the middle, and there a tower fashioned from glass and steel, in which the stone of a neighbouring building was waveringly reflected. There was an art deco 'luncheonette', and a 'movie theatre'. And the people: a tall black man in yellow robes; an Asian family walking across Fifth Avenue; a Latin-American woman with hair to her waist; a glimpse of four almost identical-looking red-haired children playing in Central Park. And the airy bulk of the Plaza Hotel, the horse-drawn carriages, the fountain: those things, those glamorous parts of New York, had not changed. They made her think of Christmas, of mittens and a long red scarf, and of her grandfather and the Russian Tea Room. Something in her, something that had lain hard and closed as a pomegranate, opened suddenly, and she began to cry, for her mother and for herself, dropping her head so the driver would not see.

On the West Side she looked out again and (surprisingly, for her) noticed food for the first time since she'd been in this taxi. She registered the many cafés, their tables sprawled festively along the sidewalks – but it was the restaurants that fairly dazzled her: upmarket and downmarket Chinese as well as noodle houses, dumpling houses and Cuban-Chinese; Indian; Thai; Vietnamese; posh Italian; modest Italian; Mexican; sushi; macrobiotic; regional American; chic French; bistro-style French; brasserie-style French;

steakhouses. And there were coffee shops galore, and pizza parlours and juice bars, Jewish delis and ice cream shops, and men selling hot-dogs from trolleys, and lots of people eating on the street. Her European self was slightly shocked to see them so informally dressed, in exercise gear or shorts, walking along Amsterdam Avenue while eating pizza or an ice cream out of their hands. But she was amused by the array of Irish bars, Blarney Stone or O'Casey's or even Blarney Rock, most of them with neon shamrocks and leprechauns in the window, something she'd never seen in Ireland.

When the taxi drew up to the hospital she fumbled in her handbag, the newly exchanged American money actually strange to her. Inside, she left her travelling things with the gruff receptionist, and went up to her mother's floor.

The corridor stank of disinfectant, with another, unwholesome smell beneath. Nurses and doctors hurried along; the intercom squawked ceaselessly and there was a general noise of machines. She found her mother's room, breathed deeply and walked in.

It was very bright, with the harshness of fluorescent lights, and loud, because the television was on. There were two beds in the room but one was empty. Her grandfather stood by her mother's bed. There were no other visitors.

When she approached, her mother turned her head on the pillow and smiled. She looked smaller, and strangely puckered, as if she were being dried. Her condition, or perhaps some medication she was on, had caused her eyes to protrude a bit, making her look slightly froglike. The smile was vague yet full of simple delight. In an unsurprised voice she said, 'Oh, Lily. I haven't seen you since this morning.'

Her grandfather touched her arm and tilted his head towards the door. When they were some distance away he murmured, 'She's quite feverish, and her ruined kidneys have poisoned her blood, so she's having delusions. She has been seeing you, and talking to you, for weeks now. They've been a comfort to her, the delusions, so I haven't challenged them. I'd advise you to play along, too.' He gave a brusque laugh. 'Thank you for coming, my dear. It's good to see you, even under these circumstances.'

They gazed at each other, they whose former complicity had excluded the woman in the bed. He also seemed smaller to her, and browner. His mottled hands looked surprisingly large in contrast to the meagre body, yet it was still a dancer's body, tough and spare, and the grey eyes were still fiercely bright. He gave her a sudden, rough kiss. 'You are beautiful as ever, but you must be so tired.'

'Exhausted.' She glanced up at the television. A car was screeching round a suburban corner; then the doors opened and four men scrambled out, waving guns. 'Isn't that awfully loud? Doesn't it disturb her?'

Again he gave a brief laugh. 'It was your father. You know how he is about television. He's only just gone down for a coffee; should be back any minute.' Once more they approached the bed. Her mother was asleep, but restively, her mouth working like an old elastic, her hand plucking at the sheet. Lily touched her dry cheek. *My mother*, she thought, marvelling at this ordinary fact, *My mother, who once carried me in her body* . . .

Her father entered the room. 'Lily,' he sighed, and kissed her. He seemed slightly ill himself; red-eyed, his dun-coloured tie askew. Just looking at him, she felt the old blend of love, exasperation and anger.

They discussed where she should stay, and agreed on her grand-father's apartment because it was convenient to the hospital. She felt relieved at the prospect of spending the evenings with Jacob, who could be difficult but was at least *connected*, as opposed to her distracted father. Even now, with his prodigal daughter newly arrived, he was gazing neither at her nor her grandfather nor his sleeping wife, but only up at the TV screen. Yet regarding his unfocused eyes and crumpled clothes, she felt a tremor of tenderness. Again, the obvious struck her like revelation, *My father; he is my father . . .* He looked at her suddenly and said, 'I'm so glad you're here, but why did you stay away so long? You could have visited us more often. Your mother has missed you.'

Lily, don't upset your mother . . . She suppressed a harsh laugh. Her grandfather eased matters by suggesting that he take her to the cafeteria for something to drink, 'since you must be dead on your feet, coming here straight off the plane.'

Later, in Jacob's apartment, after she'd had a bath and lain down briefly, he served them a light meal of cold meats and cheeses with black bread, and a tomato salad. He also opened a bottle of Beaujolais; some wine, he said, would help her sleep through the night. Since it was one o'clock in the morning as far as her interior clock was concerned, she scarcely thought she would have trouble sleeping, but accepted the wine anyway.

The apartment, like its occupant, seemed diminished to her eyes. The *Ballet-Russe* prints, the samovar and theatre properties, were all still there, but tarnished and dusty. Her grandfather, carrying a plate of cold beef to the table, walked painstakingly, and the sight of him nearly broke her heart. She wanted to kiss that brow from which the hair had receded, and to caress the face which was frowning now with concentration, as though even balancing a plate in his hands had become a challenge. And he had once been so limber that she had felt clumsy beside him. Clumsy beside him, frightened of her immense mother – and now both grandfather and mother were shrunken – as though, once again, she had grown like Alice.

They talked over the meal, a bit about her mother, but, surprisingly, more about her father. Jacob asked abruptly, 'Do you have a boyfriend, Lily?'

'Yes,' she murmured, a constriction in her throat.

Buttering some bread, Jacob said, 'Imagine, just imagine, if you and your boyfriend had a child.' Involuntarily, she curved an arm over her stomach. He went on, 'And imagine you abused this child, shouted at it or even struck it.' He looked up, with a dry smile. 'How would you feel if your boyfriend let you carry on in that way?'

She was not sure what he was getting at. 'I suppose I would feel a kind of frustration, even contempt for him. And anger. I would be angry with him for tolerating behaviour I was ashamed of, even while I was indulging in it. And for not protecting his child.'

They stared at each other. Then he continued, in a slow voice, 'I knew more about your mother's tantrums than you may think. I'd always thought they had to do with me, how I had wooed you away from her.' He paused, about to say something. Only then he shook his head and went on with his previous thought, 'But recently it occurred to me that in some important way her rages might not have been about me *or* you, not really.'

She swallowed some wine. Fatigue had plunged her into a state where everything was at once blunted, and shining with an almost hallucinatory brightness. The samovar, the red curtains and portraits of ballerinas seemed to contract and expand before her eyes. She heard from outside the ceaseless rumble of traffic, and thought of the dark ocean, and Dublin, and Nicholas. Again her arm curved round her stomach. She said, 'Are you saying she *wanted* him to stop her?'

'Something like that. I think she must have wanted to provoke *some* response from him. He was so withdrawn and passive. Only it went wrong. Instead of compelling him to *engage* with her, it had the opposite effect. She had focused her attention on you, leaving him free to withdraw even further, into whatever inward world he inhabits. Finally he could bury his head in the newspaper or gaze all evening at the TV without her bothering him, since she had you to scream at.'

Jacob let some astringency come into his voice. 'Your father, Lily, has many fine qualities. He is gentle, and honest. But he has never been imaginative or strong, and I think he let my daughter down. She must have married him for safety, after her rackety life with me. But it went wrong, as I've said. I am guessing the things which first made him attractive to her – the fact that he's so biddable and gentle – began to oppress her after a while. How would *you* feel, if you were married to somebody so timid? Who would do anything to please or appease you, anything to avoid having to get *involved* with you? So she terrorised you, in order to put some life into him.'

'Only, as you say, he was glad to be left alone. While I . . . ' She looked down at the plates.

'All I'm trying to say is, I think this may be liberating for you. To learn that it might have been more about their relationship than about you. I suspect you feel guilty, that you believe you might have deserved the terrible things she did. But you were just a little girl, Lily. Maybe it wasn't even about you.'

Before they went to bed he showed her an old photograph album. She gazed long at a photo of her mother, aged seven or eight, standing on a beach, with behind her the sinuous Jacob reclining on a blanket beside a dark-haired woman. The two adults are laughing, but little Caroline seems lonely.

'Who is that woman?' asked Lily.

'Which woman? Ah, yes.' He gave a small smile. 'I didn't remember putting that picture in here. Yes. That's Anya.'

'Who is Anya?'

He closed the album, sighing. 'Soon,' he said. 'Soon I'll tell you about Anya. But now we must go to sleep.'

They kissed good-night then, and she slept the moment her head touched the pillow of her mother's childhood bed. But towards morning she dreamt of Caroline, relaxing on a chair at a round table. She is wearing a yellow dress with a pattern of flowers, which Lily finds endearing. 'I'm so glad to see you,' Lily cries, and she is, indeed, nearly bursting with gladness.

She takes her mother's body in her arms, but sees that something is wrong; her mother is ill, her head lolling to the side. But she is not unhappy. Her eyes, despite a febrile glitter, are full of love, and she says, 'Lily, will you take the pins out of my hair, and comb it for me?'

'I will,' Lily says, sensing this is somehow important. She releases the hair into her hands, and marvels that it is so thick and bright. Then, 'Come. Eat,' says her mother. The round table is no longer bare, but laid as if for a banquet, with Levantine delicacies: figs, apricots, an amber honeycomb, bowls of nuts and olives, a white cheese moistened with oil, and bottles of dark wine. 'Come,' her mother repeats. 'It is all for us.'

A week passed, at the end of which, at dawn, her mother glided with apparent ease from sleep into death. The day before, Lily had sensed a change. She'd been alone with her mother, since most of the nurses were having their afternoon coffee break, and neither her father nor Jacob had arrived yet.

Every day so far, Caroline had received her with a gentle smile, under the impression that her daughter had never been away. One morning, in the drawer beside her mother's bed, Lily found a number of photos of herself as a baby and small girl, with her age and other details recorded in her mother's hand on the back. This afternoon, gazing out at summertime New York while Caroline slept, Lily thought she could understand how long-term patients became institutionalised. After a while, you could come to believe that this place, the whirr of its machines, its intercoms and bells, its patients in their hospital gowns, was the whole world.

Suddenly her mother opened her eyes with their new, glistering light, and said, 'Lily. Won't you give me a kiss?'

'Of course, dear.' She put down her book, and kissed her mother's forehead.

Caroline's dry hand reached out and clasped hers. Then she closed her eyes. 'Why don't you go now? I'd like to sleep.'

'All right. I'll see you tomorrow.' Yet she lingered, reluctant to leave before the nurse returned. But, eyes still closed, her mother spoke firmly. 'Go quickly,' she said.

A memory struck her with the force of unalloyed grief: her mother before a large mirror, with herself, a little girl, watching from the bed. On a table beneath the mirror, a green cup bristles with hair-pins; a comb and brush are placed neatly beside a photograph of her parents as newlyweds. While Lily gazes, Caroline raises her arms to anchor a pin in her hair; there are more pins pressed between her lips. Her eyes, meeting Lily's in the mirror, are amused, as though she means to say, 'What am I doing, standing here with pins in my mouth, fussing with my hair, on such a nice day?'

Lily was astonished that her mother should be dead, when there were just such precise memories: the watery light of the mirror, a smell of hairspray and perfume, and Caroline dressing long fair hair while her daughter gazes worshipfully at her and at both of their images in the glass.

Of course the funeral was a problem, since neither Jacob nor his daughter had ever practised any religion. But Lily and her father found themselves in agreement: there should be some kind of religious ceremony.

Lily would have preferred a proper requiem, only the sternly agnostic Jacob put his foot down at the prospect of a full-blown Catholic or Orthodox mass. So the Unitarian minister and the rabbi of Lily's suburban hometown were recruited to speak after the cremation. (Jacob hadn't particularly wanted the rabbi, but to Lily's relief he found the Unitarian minister just about acceptable.)

She listened dry-eyed to most of the ceremony, but at one point the rabbi recited Psalm 23, and when he came to the lines, '*my cup runneth over. Surely goodness and mercy shall follow me all the days of my life . . .* ' her eyes ran over with tears, and it was all she could do not to sob out loud.

She was speaking to Nicholas often. The day after her mother's death she said to him, 'I've a week here still. It's hard.'

'I know darling, believe me. How is your father? Grandfather?'

'Nick, my grandfather has a secret. For years, my mother referred to it, though always cryptically. And now I find a picture with a mysterious woman in it, and my grandfather sighs and says, "I'll tell you about her, but not now."' Lily almost said, *Both my mother and my grandfather remind me of you, the three of you alluding to secrets but never telling them,* but then she stopped herself, thinking it would be tactless to challenge him over the phone.

The morning before she was to leave, Jacob said, 'Let's have breakfast at my favourite coffee shop. Don't look so startled. One can't take *every* meal at the Russian Tea Room. Besides, this place is always full of old people like myself. Neighbourhood people. We settle at the counter and drink cup after cup of coffee, and read the *New York Times*, and gossip. Come on. They do the best breakfasts in town.'

It was exactly as he'd said, an ordinary New York coffee shop, with a long counter, steam billowing up from the coffee pots, an open grill for the cook, and mostly elderly people eating breakfast and calling greetings to one another. The postman (*mailman*, she corrected herself) had come in for a quick coffee, and the old people saluted him by name, and teased him so that he grinned and blushed. She and Jacob took two places at the counter. 'My granddaughter,' he said proudly to the white-haired woman on his other side, who exclaimed, 'Such a beauty!'

'What will you have, Lily?' he asked when the matronly waitress came, and she said, 'Poached eggs, please, on an English muffin, and tea.' Then she murmured to Jacob, 'You know, "English muffins" don't exist in England.'

'Yes, I do know. One of life's little ironies.' He smiled at the waitress. 'I'd like two fried eggs, sunny side up. They don't have "sunny side up" in England either, do they, Lily?'

'No, nor "over easy." They just say "fried eggs".'

After only a few minutes (which made Lily appreciate the meaning of 'short order cook'), the waitress set two immense oval plates in front of them, and declared, 'There you go. Farm fresh!'

'They really are,' murmured Jacob, indicating his fried eggs, whose yolks were indeed a rich, healthy-looking gold. 'They get them from a farm in New Jersey, where the hens actually live a normal life. Most American eggs are stored in warehouses for months, but not these.'

The waitress appeared yet again, to pour more coffee for Jacob, and to ask Lily, 'How are those poachers, hon?'

'Splendid,' she answered truthfully. Then she lowered her voice and said to Jacob, 'I think I'm falling in love with that woman.'

He laughed, and said, 'I'm inviting another ex-dancer, a Russian woman, for dinner tonight at the apartment. It will be just the three of us. Is that all right?'

She answered of course, and then all of a sudden he turned to face her in a way that was decisive, as if he wanted the two of them to feel they were all by themselves. And, fixing her with his seagull's gaze, he said, 'I wanted to tell you I'm sorry.'

She put down her cutlery. 'Sorry? For what?'

Again he spoke bluntly. 'For encouraging you to use your fair looks as a means to appear more romantic in the world. Perhaps such a – a strategy was not good for you, after all.

After a pause she replied, 'Well, I think it's made me feel I don't know myself. People always say, "Relax. Just be yourself." But what is oneself?' And then, haltingly, she tried to explain how she felt about her secret side; the side of her that was a fishwife, a guttersnipe. She described the aftermath of Sylvie's party, when Nicholas had endured the shrieks of the ugly creature she could become. And how when it had finally sprung forth, showing its terrible teeth, she had feared he would no longer love her.

Jacob looked stricken. 'My God,' he mumbled. 'What did I do, to make you feel that way about yourself?'

She touched his arm. He went on, 'Your poor mother. Did you hear how, during her last days, she took to calling me "Papa" again, as she'd done when she was little? "Is that you, Papa?" she'd ask when I came into the room.' He hesitated and she knew he was trying not to cry. Then he went on, 'Dear God, I sent you away from her. I divided you from her, made you into a European, made you change your class and your country, because that was what *I* wanted. I divided you, and now she's dead and it's too late.'

'I would have gone anyway,' she answered quietly. 'Even as a child I wanted to live in Europe. It's home to me now. I love my life in Ireland.' The waitress removed their plates and poured more coffee for Jacob. Lily continued, 'But perhaps I did believe I could evade my dark side by travelling to Europe and making myself into someone else there. That by living in a romantic, foreign place where I myself would be a romantic foreigner, I could escape from the past. But of course it travels within you, doesn't it? The past, and the dark side. They come with you wherever you go, don't they?'

She glanced behind the counter to where the waitress was exchanging some banter with the cook while he turned lengths of bacon on the grill. She quite liked American bacon; many of her friends in England and Ireland loved it too, although it was hard to find there.

'I was thinking I should take back some American bacon, to Nicholas. Perhaps he'd like to use it in his cooking.'

Jacob smiled. 'They may not let you take pork to Ireland. I think there's some regulation about it; Heaven knows why. But maybe you could buy him a New York delicacy, like bagels.'

She waited for him to say more, but he was silent, staring into his coffee cup. She offered, 'You know, I really couldn't change my class. They always know, the upper classes. They know by the way you lift your fork or by some inflexion in your voice. They know you aren't one of them. They just chose to forgive me, to give me a dispensation because I was a colourful foreigner.'

'And because you are beautiful.'

'Or at least peculiar-looking.'

She stayed with her father all that day, in the house of her childhood. He didn't put on the television, or read the newspaper. Mainly they reminisced, hands clasped, her head on his shoulder.

After lunch he said, 'Come out and see what I've made.'

He gestured her through the back door, where he had planted a little garden. There were roses, but also vegetables: lettuces and cabbages, and tomatoes with their heady smell.

'The salad we ate just now, it was all from here,' he said proudly. 'When I started the vegetable garden, I said to myself, Lily would love to eat home grown tomatoes, since she's so interested in food. So I planted them with you in mind.'

'Oh, Dad, thank you. They *were* delicious.' She paused. 'You know, I would love it if you came to Ireland, to visit me, once you're feeling a bit better?'

He smiled. 'We could go to Cork, where our Irish ancestors are from.'

At the station, boarding the train, she looked back at him

standing on the platform, and all of a sudden she couldn't bear it. She scrambled down again and hugged him. They stayed like that, a conventional tableau of leave-taking, until he said with a quaver in his voice, 'Hurry up, Lily, or you'll miss your train.'

The Russian ex-dancer was called Olga. She swept regally into Jacob's flat, bearing brown paper bags and talking the whole time. 'Good *evening*, my dear. I am so sorry for the loss of your daughter. Ah, life! Ah, death! And *this* is the child, the *beautiful* child. Lily, is it? Ah, Lily! Poor child!' And she kissed them both in the Continental manner before removing a number of bottles and parcels from the paper bags and placing them on the dining table.

She was about Jacob's age, Lily thought, with the face of a ruined beauty. Her eyes were a marvellous dark blue, like ink, above a prominent nose. Of course she held her fine head high, with the grey hair scraped back in ballerina style. But the skin of her cheeks and brow was heavily furrowed, and her hands, busily unwrapping packages, were gnarled with arthritis. Although Jacob had said that she'd lived in New York 'for about a thousand years', she still had a fairly thick Russian accent. And she clearly loved to talk.

'I've one bottle of *proper* salmon roe and even a bit of beluga, given me by an – ahem – friend. The rest is just lumpfish but still quite nice. And here are the lemons, Jacob, and the herrings in sour cream and the smoked salmon. The cucumber salad is in that jar, and this is a *lovely* hard cheese. And – careful! – don't let that vodka bottle fall.'

Lily asked timidly, 'May I help?' but Jacob said, 'I always leave everything to Olga. She's thoroughly at home in this kitchen, aren't you, Olga? And she always brings loads of delicious little things for our suppers. Look at that caviar! I'm meant to just supply the bread and some wine, although generally we don't make it as far as the wine.' He indicated the two large bottles of silver-blue vodka that were standing on the table.

Lily thought she'd never had such an odd and charming meal: cloudy heaps of red and black caviar with glasses of vodka; then herrings in cream sauce and smoked salmon and anchovies with the cucumber salad and more vodka. Exhausted by grief, she and Jacob were content to let Olga prattle, and Lily found her bitchy dancer's gossip amusing. Over the cheese (accompanied by yet another glass of vodka) she was saying, 'I don't know how Sonja ever thought she'd get *anywhere* in the ballet with those *hips*.' And then, 'Alex was no Nijinsky but he did jump *splendidly* in *Spectre de la Rose*. Plus that costume was *gorgeous*. One *must* admit Anya had genius.'

Lily put down her glass. 'Who is Anya?'

Her grandfather muttered, 'She was our seamstress.'

'Oh *mon Dieu*!' cried Olga, throwing up her hands. 'Seamstress is hardly the *word*! Mademoiselle Anya was an absolute *genius* with the needle. She *transformed* us into swans and roses and princes and dolls. And she was *terribly* helpful to you in your distress, Jacob, wasn't she?'

Lily stared at him. He straightened in his chair and gave her a tense smile. 'Anya was a boon to me after your grandmother died. I mean, she helped out here. She helped me to bring up your mother.'

'But why did my mother never mention her?'

There was a silence. Finally, 'Anya was devoted to me. Nothing went on between us, nothing romantic or . . . sexual. She was just one of those dutiful types. If she fastened her sense of duty on you, she would do just about anything to serve you.' He took a large gulp of vodka then grimaced. 'Only I didn't realise this sense of duty or loyalty or whatever might not extend to other members of my family. She was devoted to me, but when she was alone with Caroline . . .'

Olga thumped her two palms on the table. 'Well! I shall be off, anyway. Mustn't overstay my welcome, and I have *three* new pupils tomorrow. *Please* forgive me, darlings, for causing any awkwardness, but I absolutely *must* fly!' And then she did seem to fly out of the flat, her scarves fluttering, and her farewells like the calls of a bird. *She reminds me of Sylvie*, Lily observed in a detached way, while the rest of her churned. Yes, she was *churning*, like a pilgrim in some myth who has travelled for ages, and has at last arrived at the enchanted castle or the secret cave. Now it would be necessary to cross the threshold.

Neither Jacob nor Lily had risen from the table. Jacob muttered, 'Leave it to Olga.'

'Jacob, tell me about Anya,' said Lily quietly.

'Anya,' he said, with a sigh. 'Anya is not actually the point.' He paused; then started to speak in a measured voice as if he were telling her a children's story. Lily did not interrupt.

'Anya is not the point. The woman in my life was someone else, a lady called Laura who lived on Park Avenue. As a young girl she'd danced in the *corps de ballet* but hadn't advanced beyond it. Perhaps being rich didn't help; perhaps artists should never be *too* comfortable. However she did remain a balletomane; came to all the performances. I bumped into her outside my dressing room one evening, about two years after your grandmother died. We fell into conversation and she invited me to a late supper. Of course I was familiar with the world of the ballet, its aristocracy of talent, but also its often spurious Counts and Marquises. Laura, however, was something else, the real thing. She was from an old family – well, old by New York standards – and her apartment was full of great paintings and Louis XIV furniture.'

Lily remained silent. He went on, 'I couldn't believe my luck. I suppose I was a faux bohemian, after all. The ballet world with its *illusions* of splendour, but with such tat, greasepaint and sweat behind the lovely facades, all this had begun to exasperate me. Whereas Laura's world was genuinely beautiful, and beautifully genuine. And as *you* know better than anyone, I love beauty.'

Still Lily said nothing. He continued, 'We became lovers more or less immediately. She was also recently widowed, which deepened our connection. Mind you, I didn't abandon your mother entirely. There were times Laura travelled, or Anya was busy sewing costumes. At those times I would return, but then there would be *cascades* of visitors, people I'd neglected while I was *chez* Laura. So your mother would come home from school and find me drinking tea or vodka with Audrey or Dimitri or whoever. She was a quiet child, believe it or not. She only became overbearing later. As a little girl she was pale and quiet, and she kept to herself. When I went to kiss her goodnight I'd see that she had prepared her schoolbag and clothes for the next morning, everything placed neatly on a chair.' He took a deep breath. 'Once I noticed a bruise on her arm and I asked what had caused it. She told me she had fallen, and I probably said something fairly unkind about how clumsy she was.'

He poured them both more vodka. 'And once, when she was

quite small, she told me in a shy voice she was afraid of the corridor that lay between the kitchen and her bedroom. She was afraid to walk down it at night because of the monsters who lived there. I told her I'd escort her along that little hallway at bedtime, and we would see together there were no monsters. But of course there were; there were.'

Lily said, 'So this Anya beat her. Anything else?'

'I hope not. Caroline never told me. When she was fifteen, Anya died suddenly; a heart attack. By that time it was too late for your mother and me. She had already withdrawn.' He sighed heavily. 'Ah! But Laura . . . '

He raised his hands and examined them, the mottled backs and then the palms. 'I would wonder, when I was with Laura, was I still *me*, was it really *me* with her – tough little Jacob who'd grown up in a tenement? Was I the same person? It was an *haut bourgeois* dream, Laura's world, and I submitted to it wholly and without regret. She found children tiresome so I kept Caroline from her. And she was ever so faintly anti-Semitic. She preferred to believe I was a Russian aristocrat. And I fostered those notions; I sacrificed my daughter for them.'

A light rain had started, beating softly against the windows. He said, 'Lily, I didn't know Anya was abusing her. Or I chose not to know, until it was too late.'

'But why didn't she tell me any of this??'

'Because . . . ' His voice cracked. 'Because she was protecting me. She still loved me, after all. And she was protecting you as well, because she knew how much *you* loved me.'

He went on softly, 'When you appeared, looking so lovely, I saw you as a source of redemption for me. I pictured you conquering Europe, fulfilling my dreams but doing it honestly, through your beauty, for I had lived out a dream, all right, but in a craven way, through pretence. You, I thought, would achieve the real thing.'

In a voice soft as his own, she said, 'But you were an artist; your gift was real.' She paused. 'Anyway, I pretended, too. As you said at breakfast, you tutored me in pretence. You taught me how to use my blondeness to conceal my origins. I have lied and pretended all my adult life.'

He frowned. 'You must break the cycle, Lily. Caroline was neglected by me and abused by Anya; then she grew up to abuse you. You must break the cycle.'

'I'll try,' she said, listening to the rain falling softly on the city of her birth.

Chapter X

On her last afternoon in New York she decided to walk a bit through the city, to say a prayer for her mother at St Thomas Episcopal Church on Fifth Avenue, and drop into some exhibitions. Most important, she would make a pilgrimage to the Jewish Museum, which was showing the work of a painter she liked. She would go just to see the paintings, but also as a kind of homage: she would go for her mother and for herself.

Luckily, the heat had eased somewhat, and she could walk comfortably enough towards Fifth Avenue. Something that began to impress her, as she looked at the shops and crowds, was Manhattan's fragility. A narrow sea island, how could it support so much masonry, so much steel and iron and bustling life? The glass towers surrounding her seemed curiously insubstantial, as if they had been fashioned from air and light. Occasionally a train rumbled under her feet. It struck her that New York was a singular city, with its own rough and fragile magic.

The painter whose work was being shown at the Jewish Museum was from Kiev. Like Chagall, he had journeyed from Russia to the south of France, where, in the early years of the twentieth century, he had painted prolifically in his small studio above Nice. His work was not particularly daring, but she had always been drawn to its radiance, his way of capturing light, particularly the vivid light of the Côte d'Azur.

Only, in the museum she saw that she had underestimated him. The lovely light was there, certainly. There were pictures of purple flowers tumbling over honey-coloured walls, of ripening grapes, of the lambent curve of the Baie des Anges. But he had also achieved something more. She stopped before a painting of a Provençal balcony, a woman reclining on a chaise longue, a book in her hand, her head raised to regard the man who stands over her. It is all sunlight and colour on that terrace, the balustrade heavy with flowers, the distances solidly blue. Yet what arrested Lily was the couple, the ordinary couple, the woman dressed in white, looking up from her book, the man's expression, full of ordinary love. He is asking, *Shall we have pâté and olives for lunch, with that nice Bandol?* Or observing, *How golden your hair looks, in the sun.* And she, narrowing her fine eyes against the light, is pleased, although she affects a dryness, *How silly you are; we've been married ten years and you're still romantic as a schoolboy.*

And there was another painting, one of the few with a pronouncedly Jewish subject. A man wearing a dark beard and side curls, bathing a baby in a white pot, with a white jug beside it. In the background, a French door opens onto a glimpse of poplars. The living light cascades into the still and ordinary room. The

215

man's white sleeves are pushed up, his face soft with love; the child's round eyes look up at him in wonderment.

Yet another painting, to her the most moving of all. A yellow room, another open French door, with sun-glossed curtains. Outside, a stone terrace. It is morning. Two people lie on a rumpled bed; beside them, on a small table, are the remains of their breakfast: two white bowls, shiny as eggs, two little white jugs, two plates with crumbs and knives, a pot of honey. The woman wears a blue nightdress; she has a small face, very pretty, with large dark eyes and pale, slightly olive skin. Her dark head is cradled on the man's shoulder; she is looking up at the ceiling with a dreamy expression. The man, handsome in an aquiline way, wearing white pyjama bottoms, his brown chest bare, also gazes at the ceiling, on which, one suspects, the sunlight is making patterns. It is clear from their faces and general languor that they are talking idly, affectionately, their words mingling and blurring with the sunlight. They are happy. It is, once again, an ordinary moment.

She recalled the morning after Sylvie's party, how she had concluded, with a sour certainty, that a real understanding between lovers was not possible. But the man and woman on their sun-warmed bed reproached her now. She was sensing something deeper beneath the tender moment: probably they have just made love; their repose and *dishabille* suggest it. But their conversation, while they gaze at the ceiling, is obviously as intimate, perhaps more so, than the sexual coupling that preceded it. I understand now, she thought. The spirit and the body blending in joy, the knowledge of another which is also an understanding of one's self, the journey one makes into the heart of things, with the beloved, through physical pleasure, through intimacies shyly revealed on a tousled bed, through talk and shared silences. Her black hair curls on his naked shoulder, sunlight shines on a white bowl. The room *must* smell of coffee and oranges. The man and women are their separate selves but they are also together; and they *are* the smell of oranges, the sunlight, the yellow curtains. The carnal and the spiritual lie together on that bed; the room is full of love.

Her vision blurred with a kind of gratitude. It was as though her mother were with her, a faint shadow upon the air; a smell like a crushed flower. She remembered Jacob saying, *You must break the cycle.*

Walking out into the afternoon, she felt curiously light-headed. Central Park was crowded with cyclists, and children holding balloons. She walked in the opposite direction, eastwards to Park Avenue, where she stopped, on one of the islands in the middle, to look downtown.

Either it was a sluggish time of day, or else here, on upper Park Avenue, one was far enough away from the commercial district to escape its clamour. For a moment not a single car moved along or across the avenue, and there was no one other than herself on foot. She was alone on this measure of Park Avenue, gazing down its broad expanse: that procession of flower boxes on the little islands, the formal houses giving way, further downtown, to glass skyscrapers, the bulk of what she had known as the Pan Am Building, but which was now called something else, concealing the baroque facade of Grand Central Station. Once more she was struck by how fragile they looked, those glass buildings that had been built to celebrate commerce, prowess; how fragile, reflecting the clouds . . .

The afternoon was nearly as balmy as spring, with a powdery quality to the light. Along one of the bisecting roads, children were clustered on the stoop of a brownstone: she had forgotten that New York word, *stoop*, from the Dutch. She was too distant to be sure, but it seemed they were playing marbles. Listening to their faint cries, she suddenly had the odd sensation that she was, literally, full of light. A kind of glow seemed to course along her face and body, and to cascade out through her fingertips. She looked again down the undulant sweep of avenue, at the flowers and elegant houses. Soon taxis, cars and bicycles would re-appear, along with pedestrians who would stop at the corners and scowl into the traffic, waiting for the light to change. But for a moment everything was empty, quiet and shining.

★

She slept briefly on the flight to Dublin. But mostly she stared out of the window, at her own face reflected against the black sky, unable to concentrate on the novel she had bought that morning, or to eat the less than enticing dinner. *They should just have picnics on planes*, she said to herself, covertly examining her neighbour's meal, *they should just have nice bits of ham, and pâté and cornichons, and cheese, and good bread, instead of that truly scary-looking stew.*

She was eager to arrive, and had begun to really miss Dublin. But more urgently, of course, she was missing Nicholas. Gazing out of the window as dawn broke over the horizon of Europe, she murmured a prayer.

He was standing in the middle of the terminal, a bag of Odlum's flour in his arms.

'It's my way of giving flowers.' Then, with his wry smile, 'Not really. Just thought it would be funny.'

'It *is* funny.'

'I missed you,' he said simply, and they kissed.

They began to walk out towards his car. It had been raining; the tarmac glistened and the wind was fresh. He said, 'It's good timing you came back on my day off. I hope you didn't eat breakfast. I was up very early and made bread, and yesterday I bought fresh raspberries and fromage blanc.'

On the drive into town he continued, in the nearly feverish way he always talked about food, 'For lunch I thought I'd make quenelles de brochet, but not with the usual seafood sauce. I was thinking of something more fragrant, something with herbs. Chives maybe? And a green salad. Nothing too heavy, since you must be exhausted. We might have that soft Italian cheese and more berries, for dessert?'

'Nicholas, I love you,' she said.

They were silent a while. She was happy despite her grief, happy for his presence beside her, for the rain-washed sky, for the Royal Canal and the green buses and people on bicycles.

In the flat he began to prepare breakfast. She looked at the familiar kitchen with its hanging ropes of garlic, and its pots of basil and rosemary on the counter. 'Nicholas,' she sighed, putting her arms around him, and then they forgot about breakfast.

Presently, her eyes opened on a different light, and she knew she had slept for hours and it was now afternoon. She reached out but his side of the bed was empty, and for a moment she was cold with fear. Where had he gone? Where was *she*, for that matter? Had she really flown back to Dublin or was this still her mother's old bed in Jacob's apartment? Perhaps she had merely dreamt her return. In an urgent voice she called out, '*Nicholas*'.

He came hurrying in from the kitchen. There was a dollop of cream on his nose.

She began to laugh. 'Sorry. Sorry to alarm you. Nothing's wrong. Nothing at all.'

Two evenings later, after eating on assignment at a chichi new bistro in Ranelagh, she went to see Nicholas at the Matisse. She liked to go there late, when the dining room had that mysterious air common to public places after the public has left: the candles blown out, tables silent, the waiters and kitchen staff talking lazily up at the bar. Although tonight Nicholas was alone; it had been a slow evening so he'd sent everyone home early.

He was sitting at a corner table, reading a cookery book, a glass of red wine at his elbow. 'Look at this,' he said. 'This recipe for sea bass stuffed with ham and prunes. Now *there's* a dish that could be either delicious or else truly revolting.'

She helped herself to some of his wine. 'Lovely. A Burgundy, is it?'

He rose to fetch a glass for her. 'Yes, a really good Burgundy, but too dear, it seems. The boss says we can't order it again. Tonight he spoke to me in that solemn voice he always uses to talk about money: "*You know, Nicholas, this boom won't last forever.*" He's right. It won't last forever.'

They were silent, fingers laced across the table. Lily said, 'The magazine wants me to go to Belfast the day after tomorrow. Seems it's bulging with good restaurants these days, a new Belfast for the new millennium. Actually, they'd like me to do a whole series on

Northern Irish food, as well. Not things like your mother's brutal fries, but the good traditional dishes.' She paused. '*Are* there any good traditional dishes?'

He laughed. 'There's fish from Loch Neagh and eels from the Bann. And some good potato things, potato bread and boxty, and champ made with loads of butter and salt and green onions. There's even a Northern poem about champ.' He cleared his throat before reciting:

> *And she up with the beetle,*
> *And she broke the lamp,*
> *And then she had room,*
> *For to beetle the champ.*

He laughed again. 'It's about a woman trying to cook in a very wee house.'

'What in Heaven's name is a beetle?

'A wooden pounding thing to crush the potatoes.' He frowned. 'I can't remember any other Northern dishes at the moment.' Lighting a cigarette, he went on softly, 'You know, I think I might be curious to see Belfast again.'

Yet again they were silent. There was a low sound of traffic from the road below. Lily said, 'Why don't you come up with me? Couldn't your sous chef take over for one day? We could drive up to Belfast and have dinner and drive home the same evening. Besides, I have something to tell you, and I would like to tell you there, in Belfast.'

'Well,' he said, 'well.' He was smiling down at the table. 'I suppose I have things to tell you, too.'

Traffic was light and so in less than an hour they arrived at a particular valley Nicholas had wanted her to see. He'd said he preferred it to other ancient parts of Meath like Tara, perhaps because it was less well known.

So after driving along the Ashbourne Strait, he turned the car onto a narrow road until they came to this valley where they were the only people.

It was one of those Irish mornings that hover between rain and sunlight, the air blurring, then shining and then blurring again. The sky was oyster-coloured, with intermittent splashes of blue; the hedges were pearled with incipient rain, and the wind smelled of wet leaves and turf smoke. Slowly they walked to the centre of the valley where the ruins of an abbey and a High Cross stood.

While her eyes followed its raised images – diminutive prophets, magi, Virgins and Christs – Nicholas said, 'This cross is probably from the eighth century, much older than the Roman church in Ireland. This is the real Celtic thing. It gives you an idea as to how they worshipped, before the Normans came.'

While they walked back to the car, she asked how he felt about Celtic Ireland, since his own ancestry, the genetic stuff of him, was different.

He snorted. 'Oh, *genes*. Who cares? We're all interwoven, like the designs on that Cross. I'm so tired of everyone going on the whole time about "identity". There's no such thing as this kind of people or that kind of people. There's just *people*.'

It was a phantom border, Lily thought. In the past there would have
been checkpoints, and soldiers dressed absurdly in jungle camou-
flage, and helicopters thumping overhead. But now they simply
drove through the terrain of Ireland, under the windblown Irish
sky, with nothing to indicate any kind of border except that the
signposts were suddenly identical to those Lily had known in the
England of her youth, the same font, with no Irish underneath. The
only other startling things were the spidery mesh of a now-empty
watch tower standing forlornly on top of Sliabh Gullion, and the
sudden profusion of petrol stations.

Nicholas said, 'Sometimes Catholic petrol is cheaper; sometimes Protestant. So people come and go across the border.'

After this half-joke, he was largely silent, concentrating on driving, his lips set. Lily, who had just come back from a voyage to her
own fraught birthplace, knew better than to disturb him as they
journeyed towards his. But then all of a sudden she was dreadfully
hungry. Those odd symptoms, which had largely disappeared during her visit to New York, had come back in force on her return to
Ireland: an aversion to foods she usually loved, a fierce desire for
bizarre things like avocadoes with mayonnaise or a whole bottle of
sour gherkins, and sometimes nausea followed by a hunger so powerful, it made her dizzy. She said, 'Nick, could we stop for lunch?
I'm famished. Could we stop in this town?'

'Not here,' he said tightly. She looked out of the window and
saw Union Jacks draped over the pubs and houses, and red, white
and blue banners fastened to the lamp posts. 'They've even painted
the kerbs,' said Nicholas in that same tight voice, 'just so you won't

forget what side you're supposed to be on, even when you're looking down.'

'Well,' said Lily weakly, 'I suppose it's meant to be – festive?'

He laughed, and said nothing more.

The restaurant, on a leafy street close to Queen's University, was
quite a la mode, with umber lighting, camel-coloured banquettes,
and very pretty waitresses wearing the upmarket bistro uniform of
tight-little-black-dress-and-black-heels.

'I feel all rumpled,' Lily said. 'Perhaps we should have brought
a change of clothes in the car?'

'Never mind.' Nicholas gave his half-frown, half-smile. 'It's
only Belfast.'

She regarded him over the menus. 'Well, *this* bit of Belfast looks
quite charming, like a Victorian English provincial city. I can't say
what I think *your* bit of Belfast looks like, because I haven't seen it
yet.'

'Hmm. This ravioli thing stuffed with confit de canard would
make a nice starter.'

She was silent. Finally he lowered the menu and said, 'Not now.
Not this visit. You said you'll be coming back to do your Northern
food series, so perhaps we'll go then and see the house where I grew
up. But just being back in this town is about as much as I can take
tonight.' He glanced round at the other diners, mainly young or
youngish women, all of whom seemed to be blonde and gleaming,
accompanied by young or youngish men wearing suits or expen-
sive-looking jerseys. 'Though I can't say I recognise anything. I

suppose Belfast is beginning to look like every other city. Or at least its restaurant scene is.' Lily smiled, wondering, as she often wondered in Dublin, where all the lovely Irish auburn and russet hair had gone, along with pale skin and cinnamon-coloured freckles: nearly everyone in the room looked as if they'd just returned from the Costa del Sol.

Nicholas said, 'So why don't you order the ravioli thing and I'll have the calamari thing.'

'And afterwards you take the wild boar sausage and I'll choose – let's see – something fishy, I think.'

'The brown trout with thyme and juniper berries,' he said promptly. 'You wouldn't mind drinking red wine with trout, would you?'

'Heavens, no. I love red wine with everything.'

After they had ordered and were drinking the wine, there was a change in the atmosphere, a kind of deepening or concentration. Lily was reminded of her last night in Jacob's flat; she had felt, then, a similar charge in the air. They gazed at each other, and Nicholas said, 'So, no more distractions. Shall I go first?'

★

He was only nineteen when he left. He hadn't considered London, even though it offered more opportunities for a fledgling chef. He was tired of his neighbours insisting on their 'Britishness': he wanted to live in an Ireland that was merely Irish, so he went to Dublin.

He found a flat in the flat-cluttered Rathmines of that period. It was small and fairly squalid, with distempered walls and noisy neighbours, and his job as commis chef in a primitive Italian restaurant (overcooked spaghetti and rough red wine) was menial and boring. But he didn't mind. He had already modified his Northern accent and had found work in an actual restaurant. He was, he thought, changing his life.

It was 1974. Except for the burning of the British Embassy in Dublin two years before and a few other nasty though relatively minor incidents, the Republic was having very little direct experience of the Troubles. The television news was full of bomb blasts and weeping or angry families, but it was all going on *up there*, the place he had left behind. Anyway, he was interested in food, not politics – also there was a pretty redhead who lived in a nearby flat and who looked at him a fraction of a second longer than necessary when they greeted each other in the street or the pub, which encouraged him to think he could invite her for a drink or to the cinema.

Only one day in May, his distant cousin David arrived, unannounced. David was considerably older than Nicholas, nearly as old as Nicholas's father. Nicholas had a vague impression that he worked in a factory, but they had never been close.

Yet now David had come to Dublin, 'for a bit of fresh air', and was expecting to stay with Nicholas, who felt unable to refuse, although he was dismayed. He was dismayed because his cousin embodied everything he had been trying to escape from by coming South. David was small, burly and rooster-like. He was also uncouth, sweaty, unshaven and badly dressed. He wore unbecoming round spectacles, of which one of the wings had been mended with sellotape. He spoke in a loud bellicose way and, worst of all, in a pronounced Belfast accent. But he was only staying for a week and, besides, he was family.

And to Nicholas's relief, he wasn't intrusive. He had come with a sleeping bag, pillow, a box of Lyon's tea and a clutch of Dublin guidebooks, which were all he seemed to desire or need. Nicholas was a bit puzzled but also amused by the scholarly way he prepared for his forays into the city, spreading those guidebooks over the table each evening, and examining them narrowly while nibbling on a pencil. He left in the morning and returned just as Nicholas was going out to work. All in all, he seemed intensely solitary, except for one evening early in the week when a tall man with an English accent called for him and they went briefly to the pub. In any case, Nicholas, absorbed with the restaurant and with his pursuit of the redhead, was happy to leave David to his own devices.

On the seventeenth of May, at about two in the afternoon, David bundled the sleeping bag back into his rucksack and left for Belfast. He was vague about how he would travel: the bus was cheaper but the train pleasanter.

Nicholas accompanied him down to the street. 'I could come with you to Busáras or Connolly Station, whichever one you choose?'

'Ach, don't bother. I'll manage.' He squeezed Nicholas's shoulder and said something about not letting the Taigs get him down, which was the only sectarian remark he'd made all week. Then he was gone.

At half past five or so that evening, Nicholas was having a bath in the not-so-clean communal bathroom when there was a sudden din outside on the landing: people shouting, and the sobbing voice of his landlady. He clambered out of the bath, dragged on his dressing gown and, still soaking wet, opened the door upon his two fellow tenants, one a student, the other a commercial traveller, both talking loudly while trying to place a consoling hand on the arm of Mrs Mulvaney, who was clutching at her hair and keening.

When they finally noticed Nicholas, the student told him what Mrs Mulvaney had just seen on the television. Moments before, at the height of the rush hour and without warning, three car bombs had exploded in Dublin. Later, Nicholas would learn the following:

The bombs had gone off on Parnell Street, Talbot Street and South Leinster Street. The Talbot Street car had been stolen that morning from the Belfast Docks, while the other two had been hijacked, also that same morning.

Taking into account the fourth car bomb that would go off about an hour later in Monaghan, more people died or were injured on the seventeenth of May, 1974, than on any other single day of the Troubles.

Most of the victims were women. Many were girls from country towns who worked in the civil service. Some were trudging homewards along streets that were unusually crowded, because a bus strike was on. One was a French Jew whose family had perished in the Holocaust. Another was nine months pregnant, and so her unborn child would be considered a victim as well, raising the death toll from thirty-three to thirty-four.

The redhead from Nicholas's street, who worked behind a perfume counter at Guineys department store, was struck by shrapnel and lost both of her green eyes.

★

Once more, on instinct, Lily's arm had curved protectively over her stomach. Nicholas continued in a dogged voice, 'I must give you some background. I should tell you what was going on then, in the North.'

And so he spoke about the Sunningdale Agreement, and the Northern Ireland Assembly, and the frail hope that lay behind those things, for power sharing between Nationalists and Unionists in the North, and also between Northern Ireland and the Republic. And he told her how violently the hard line Unionists had opposed Sunningdale, going so far as to organise the Ulster Workers' Council Strike, and how the Ulster Volunteer Force had wanted to scare the Republic into withdrawing support for the Agreement by bombing Dublin and Monaghan on the seventeenth of May.

'And they weren't alone,' he said. 'The UVF weren't operating alone. They had help from the British security forces, I'm sure of it. That was why the only person David met socially during his bizarre stay in Dublin was a man with an English accent.'

She asked slowly, 'David was in the UVF?'

'Or some other organisation beginning with "U", though I don't think he and Martin were ever connected. Anyhow, David was never convicted or even suspected. In fact no one has ever been prosecuted for those massacres. But he was killed a few years later, by an IRA bomb.' He laughed bleakly. 'I suppose what goes around, comes around. At least sometimes.'

The waitress served their starters, and Lily ate mechanically, realising only when she was staring down at an empty plate that she'd registered nothing, neither flavour nor texture nor sauce nor garnish, for the first time in her professional life. In confusion she swept her eyes over this blandly chic room, so different from the Belfast Nicholas had known and out of which his brother and uncle David had emerged, thinking she'd have to ask the waitress to give her a list of the ingredients. And at the same time she was trembling, *trembling*. For not only had Nicholas's secret upset her in itself, it had also made her more afraid to reveal her own. What must he feel now, about family, the *fact* of it? She had a sudden memory of Hugo, how his eyes would turn wintry when he was displeased. Her arm curved yet again over her belly. And she trembled.

Nicholas said, 'I think he must have come to Dublin on a reconnaissance mission, something like that. But I never for one moment really *thought* about it. I never asked myself why he was studying those street plans of Dublin with the concentration of a scholar. I never asked what he was doing in the Republic in the first place, Taig-hating bigot that he was. "A bit of fresh air," he'd told me, and I just accepted it. I let him stay, and survey the scene, and tell that shit from MI5 where the cars should be left.'

'You aren't certain, Nicholas. This is just surmise. And you were a young man, intent on your own young life. You did nothing wrong.'

Oblivious, he went on, 'I feel like those people who harbour a disease without showing any symptoms. What are they called? Carriers? I feel like a carrier, harbouring David and passing on his evil to other people, while remaining unscathed myself.'

As if she'd sensed they were engrossed in an important exchange, the waitress reappeared to ask, 'Would you like to wait a wee while before I serve the main course?' to which they answered 'Yes, please. Thank you,' in unison. And after she'd gone, Nicholas gave his wry smile again and murmured, 'How gracious they've become, the Belfast lot, while I was away.'

Lily repeated firmly, 'You did nothing wrong.' She took a deep breath. 'But by scourging yourself like this, by making yourself into a scapegoat, you are behaving like the people you decry, like Martin and David and all the others in those organisations beginning with "U" or "I".' She reached for his hand. 'Nick, listen to me. You condemn those people because they are hard-hearted and intolerant and cruel. But you are behaving like them, towards your own self. And you must *stop*. You must finally stop lacerating yourself because— '

She fell silent. Nicholas said, 'Why?'

Again she breathed deeply. 'Because I think we weren't careful enough. I think – I think I'm pregnant.'

Now it was his turn to be silent. She continued hurriedly, 'I'm not completely sure. And I'm not saying I've made up my mind about what to do. I mean, we were both fairly unhappy as children; perhaps we wouldn't want to bring another child into the world. We could always, you know, go to Liverpool or something.'

After a moment, he squeezed her hand across the table.

Later, Lily would remember what they had eaten. In retrospect, she found herself savouring the ravioli, one large square of slightly golden pasta, clearly made with good hard flour and eggs, and cooked 'to the tooth', which Lily appreciated since she detested soggy pasta. It was full of the rich meat of cuisse de canard confite, and served in a sauce of duck broth thickened with cream. And

Nicholas's calamari, encrusted with salt and pepper and dry-cooked in the pan, were tender, which Lily also appreciated since she disliked food that had lost the texture of food and reminded one of something else: like rubbery calamari. Indeed, this was why she absolutely abhorred fruit jellies. As for her trout, it had been cooked in a simple reduction of fresh thyme and juniper, which rendered it so tender and herbaceous, and so colourful, she thought it must be the nicest trout she had ever tasted.

Epilogue

Le Café de Nice
Dun Laoghaire
by Lily Murphy

I must declare a bias. I love Nice, even if time has tarnished
its former splendour. No longer do aristocrats stroll ceremo-
niously along the Promenade des Anglais while great artists
paint the blazing light in their eyries above the town. At first
Nice was merely beautiful; then it grew popular, then spoilt
until finally it was abandoned by the fashionable because it
had become louche. Which, in a way, meant a curving back,
an unspoiling.

The Nice I love (I went there first as a girl, and, more
recently, on my honeymoon) is pretty much a market town,
full of coughing motor cars, cafés and people with scarves
wound about their necks and cigarettes dangling from their
mouths. Full, in fact, of the usual Gallic clichés. What makes
it different from many other French towns is, of course, the

presence of the Mediterranean, the olive and palm trees, an occasional smell of lavender in the air, the Italianate architecture – and the food.

The cours saleya in Nice is beautiful, with its canopies fluttering in the salt light. And the food on display there, much of it brought down from the mountains just north of the city, is unusual and delicious, like those strong mushrooms called sanguins with their smell of the loam in which they were fostered, and porous cheeses made from the milk of mountain goats, alongside hams and saucisses de sanglier from Corsica.

And there are plenty of fine, modest restaurants in Nice, especially Old Nice, where one can savour the delicacies of the region for a pittance. The city was originally part of Italy; in fact, Garibaldi was born there, and its earlier name was Nizza. Italy remains part of Nice's culinary heritage, with pastas, pizzas, tomato sauces, and sauces redolent of olive oil and garlic appearing on almost every restaurant menu. A North African influence also endures, in dishes like socca, a savoury pancake made from chickpea flour.

Le Café de Nice is gratifyingly authentic. I know 'authenticity' is considered a debatable virtue these days, but it was very pleasant to walk into a room so simply evocative of the south of France. Of course, the restaurant is not entirely responsible for its Mediterranean atmosphere: its broad windows overlook the sea, so that on a fine day the place shimmers with a marine light. But the furnishings are charmingly Provençal, even if they do border on the kitsch: wooden tables with flowered cloths and jugs of flowers, farm implements against the rough walls, a board where the tarts and cheeses are displayed. All in all, an appealing and unpretentious dining room.

The food is charming too, a tribute to Provençal cookery and especially the dishes of Nice. One may begin with salade niçoise, a rather offbeat version since it features a gently poached rather than the usual hard-boiled egg. But I must admit this turns out to be a good variation, since the yolk flows into the vinaigrette and enriches it. And the tuna is fresh and lightly cooked; the vegetables colourful and crunchy. Or there is pissaladière, the niçoise tart of onions, olives and anchovies, delicious though fiercely thirst-inducing. You may also start with that old standby, ratatouille, one of those dishes which can be superb, but is more often poorly executed. How often have you eaten a sodden vegetable stew, masquerading as ratatouille? (Recently, in a Wicklow restaurant, I was served a mess of overcooked vegetables – including *mushrooms* and *cauliflower* – drenched in a musty-smelling murk that had clearly been poured from a bottle of spaghetti sauce.) Let me hasten to say the ratatouille offered here is excellent, a succulent melange of onions, red and green peppers, courgettes, aubergines and tomatoes, bound in an almost ethereal sauce fragrant with garlic and herbs. The simple traditional starter of grilled peppers is good as well, especially with the restaurant's thick-crusted bread. Le Café de Nice also offers les petits farcis: red peppers, courgettes and aubergines stuffed with veal and herbes de Provence, another homely regional dish. Nice's homage to Italy is evident in the very pleasant starter of jambon cru and salami, accompanied by a dry sheep's cheese that is similar to parmesan but stronger; and in the gnocchis niçois, which in Nice are known by a highly amusing name that, unfortunately, I am not allowed to print in this family magazine.

Le Café de Nice is lovely at lunch on a fine day, when that clean light glows on the walls and wineglasses, and you can hear a faint clang from the moored boats just outside in the harbour. And nearly any one of the starters described above could serve as a midday meal, since the portions are ample. On the other hand, it would be a pity to miss the fine main courses, which include daube de boeuf, a luscious if heavy casserole of beef, bacon and red wine. There is also aioli de cabillaud et ses legumes, the traditional Friday dish of Nice but served every day here. It is a simple preparation: poached cod with carrots, potatoes, leeks and cauliflower and half a hard-boiled egg. Admittedly, this would be an insipid plate of food – if it were not for the aioli itself, that mayonnaise richly seasoned with garlic. Other main courses include brandade de morue (salt cod mixed with garlicky mashed potatoes); soupe de poissons (usually a starter in Nice, but served here as a rather vast main course, with the traditional accompaniments of croûtes, a pot of crumbled parmesan and another of rouille); roast dourade; grilled sardines; tripeaux niçoise (tripe cooked in a spicy tomato sauce); and roast chicken with whole cloves of roasted garlic. All were excellent when we tried them on various nights, even when the restaurant was crowded.

There is an extraordinary dessert of the region, a cake made with Swiss chard, or blettes, a startling thought, like trying to envisage artichoke ice cream or calf's liver sorbet. After all, chard is a bitter green, a kind of tougher spinach, and the uninitiated would not automatically associate it with the pudding course. Yet, boiled, sweetened and spread between two layers of crumbly pastry, it is delicious. The tourte de blettes served here is exceptional, as are the fruit tarts with their frangible crusts, and the homemade ice creams.

Rosés are generally not the most distinguished wines, but the rosés of Provence are pleasantly piquant, and lovely with the area's highly spiced dishes. Three are featured here, all fine. Everyone knows about Côtes du Rhône, but this restaurant features a smooth Bouches du Rhône, straight from the river's mouth, as well as a dark Bandol, and a number of modestly priced Côtes de Provence, white and red. None of the bottles is overpriced, and the vins de maison, presumably direct from the Var, are a superb value.

In addition to the good food and relatively low prices, Le Café de Nice throws a great party. Not long ago, some friends organised a gathering here, to celebrate my marriage to the chef Nicholas Savage. The restaurant responded with tremendous style, producing a meal so sumptuous, it dazzled even the veteran foodies in our group, including not only Nicholas, but Count Bartholomew O'Sullivan-Kelly (dining-out columnist for *Emerald Isle*), and our friends Theo, Will, Sylvie, Lucien, Didier and the artist Orla Smith, all dyed-in-the-wool gourmets.

We began with pastis, of course, accompanied by miniature pissaladières and bouchees aux fruits de mer, as well as prawns with pots of mayonnaise, and rounds of goat's cheese marinated in olive oil and herbs. And these were only morsels, or amuses geules, to sharpen our appetite for the starter, a superb crayfish terrine. Good champagne appeared alongside in fragile flutes, as if by magic.

The fish course was loup de mer in a seafood sauce, accompanied by a white Côtes de Provence. And there were also blini with black caviar, a homage to the Russian influence in Nice. (The Russian church in Nice is marvellous, its domes exuberantly colourful. And since my own ancestry is partly Russian, and my grandfather a former ballet dancer with whom I grew up eating blini and caviar, this part of the meal held a special delight for me.)

After blackberry sorbet, the main course arrived, magret de canard, served in a sauce of Provençal honey. The bottles of Chateau d'Aigueville that accompanied this went down very well.

The proprietor confided that the fromages were not of the region, since Provence is one of the few areas of France not distinguished by its cheeses, but they were more than satisfactory, as was the Coteaux d'Aix with which they were served. Dessert, blessedly, was light: pruneaux soaked in red wine and perfumed with cinnamon. A plate of petits-fours and deliciously bitter black chocolates appeared with the fine coffee.

This was an unabashedly sybaritic feast; we ate and drank and lingered at table until dawn broke over the harbour. That was a lovely moment: the mother of pearl sky, the faint sound of clonking boats, the drowsy faces round the table. Such moments are rare, when one has eaten and drunk too much, yet is neither uncomfortably full nor drunk, when one has been up all night and is not tired, when one has been, perhaps, excessive, without suffering from excess. Perhaps it is affection that leavens such times, a balance between material things and the life of the heart, so that the pleasures of the table become a means for other kinds of rejoicing. We can feel light while enjoying abundance: we have used, not abused, the fruits of the earth.